STRIFE AND OTHER PLAYS

JOHN GALSWORTHY

Black Box Press
Arlington, TX

NOTE: The plays in this volume are in the public domain and may be performed without paying royalties.

ISBN 978-0-6152-1276-0

First Black Box Press Edition

CONTENTS

———•—————

STRIFE

A DRAMA IN THREE ACTS

CHARACTERS

JOHN ANTHONY, Chairman of the Trenartha Tin Plate Works
EDGAR ANTHONY, his Son

FREDERIC H. WILDER
WILLIAM SCANTLEBURY • Directors Of the same
OLIVER WANKLIN

HENRY TENCH, Secretary of the same
FRANCIS UNDERWOOD, C.E., Manager of the same
SIMON HARNESS, a Trades Union official

DAVID ROBERTS
JAMES GREEN
JOHN BULGIN,   • The workmen's committee
HENRY THOMAS
GEORGE ROUS

HENRY ROUS
LEWIS
JAGO
EVANS   • Workmen at the Trenartha Tin Plate Works
A BLACKSMITH
DAVIES
A RED-HAIRED YOUTH
BROWN

FROST, valet to John Anthony
ENID UNDERWOOD, Wife of Underwood, daughter of John Anthony
ANNIE ROBERTS, wife of David Roberts
MADGE THOMAS, daughter of Henry Thomas
MRS. ROUS, mother of George and Henry Rous
MRS. BULGIN, wife of John Bulgin
MRS. YEO, wife of a workman
A PARLOURMAID to the Underwoods
JAN, Madge's brother, a boy of ten
A CROWD OF MEN ON STRIKE

STRIFE

ACT I. The dining-room of the Manager's house.

[The action takes place on February 7th between the hours of noon and six in the afternoon, close to the Trenartha Tin Plate Works, on the borders of England and Wales, where a strike has been in progress throughout the winter.]

[It is noon. In the Underwoods' dining-room a bright fire is burning. On one side of the fireplace are double-doors leading to the drawing-room, on the other side a door leading to the hall. In the centre of the room a long dining-table without a cloth is set out as a Board table. At the head of it, in the Chairman's seat, sits JOHN ANTHONY, an old man, big, clean-shaven, and high-coloured, with thick white hair, and thick dark eyebrows. His movements are rather slow and feeble, but his eyes are very much alive. There is a glass of water by his side. On his right sits his son EDGAR, an earnest-looking man of thirty, reading a newspaper. Next him WANKLIN, a man with jutting eyebrows, and silver-streaked light hair, is bending over transfer papers. TENCH, the Secretary, a short and rather humble, nervous man, with side whiskers, stands helping him. On WANKLIN'S right sits UNDERWOOD, the Manager, a quiet man, with a long, stiff jaw, and steady eyes. Back to the fire is SCANTLEBURY, a very large, pale, sleepy man, with grey hair, rather bald. Between him and the Chairman are two empty chairs.]

WILDER: *[Who is lean, cadaverous, and complaining, with drooping grey moustaches, stands before the fire.]* I say, this fire's the devil! Can I have a screen, Tench?

SCANTLEBURY: A screen, ah!

TENCH: Certainly, Mr. Wilder. *[He looks at UNDERWOOD.]* That is-- perhaps the Manager--perhaps Mr. Underwood----

SCANTLEBURY: These fireplaces of yours, Underwood----

UNDERWOOD: *[Roused from studying some papers.]* A screen? Rather! I'm sorry. *[He goes to the door with a little smile.]* We're not accustomed to complaints of too much fire down here just now.

[He speaks as though he holds a pipe between his teeth, slowly, ironically.]

WILDER: *[In an injured voice.]* You mean the men. H'm!
[UNDERWOOD goes out.]

SCANTLEBURY: Poor devils!

WILDER: It's their own fault, Scantlebury.

EDGAR: *[Holding out his paper.]* There's great distress among them, according to the Trenartha News.

WILDER: Oh, that rag! Give it to Wanklin. Suit his Radical views. They call us monsters, I suppose. The editor of that rubbish ought to be shot.

EDGAR: *[Reading.]* "If the Board of worthy gentlemen who control the Trenartha Tin Plate Works from their arm-chairs in London would condescend to come and see for themselves the conditions prevailing amongst their work-people during this strike----"

WILDER: Well, we have come.

EDGAR: *[Continuing.]* "We cannot believe that even their leg-of-mutton hearts would remain untouched."
[WANKLIN takes the paper from him.]

WILDER: Ruffian! I remember that fellow when he hadn't a penny to his name; little snivel of a chap that's made his way by black-guarding everybody who takes a different view to himself.
[ANTHONY says something that is not heard.]

WILDER: What does your father say?

EDGAR: He says "The kettle and the pot."

WILDER: H'm!
[He sits down next to SCANTLEBURY.]

SCANTLEBURY: *[Blowing out his cheeks.]* I shall boil if I don't get that screen.

[UNDERWOOD and ENID enter with a screen, which they place before the fire. ENID is tall; she has a small, decided face, and is twenty-eight years old.]

ENID: Put it closer, Frank. Will that do, Mr. Wilder? It's the highest we've got.

WILDER: Thanks, capitally.

SCANTLEBURY: *[Turning, with a sigh of pleasure.]* Ah! Merci, Madame!

ENID: Is there anything else you want, Father? *[ANTHONY shakes his head.]* Edgar--anything?

EDGAR: You might give me a "J" nib, old girl.

ENID: There are some down there by Mr. Scantlebury.

SCANTLEBURY: *[Handing a little box of nibs.]* Ah! your brother uses "J's." What does the manager use? *[With expansive politeness.]* What does your husband use, Mrs. Underwood?

UNDERWOOD: A quill!

SCANTLEBURY: The homely product of the goose. *[He holds out quills.]*

UNDERWOOD: *[Drily.]* Thanks, if you can spare me one. *[He takes a quill.]* What about lunch, Enid?

ENID: *[Stopping at the double-doors and looking back.]* We're going to have lunch here, in the drawing-room, so you needn't hurry with your meeting.
[WANKLIN and WILDER bow, and she goes out.]

SCANTLEBURY: *[Rousing himself, suddenly.]* Ah! Lunch! That hotel— Dreadful! Did you try the whitebait last night? Fried fat!

WILDER: Past twelve! Aren't you going to read the minutes, Tench?

TENCH: *[Looking for the CHAIRMAN'S assent, reads in a rapid and monotonous voice.]* "At a Board Meeting held the 31st of January at the

Company's Offices, 512, Cannon Street, E.C. Present—Mr. Anthony in the chair, Messrs. F. H. Wilder, William Scantlebury, Oliver Wanklin, and Edgar Anthony. Read letters from the Manager dated January 20th, 23d, 25th, 28th, relative to the strike at the Company's Works. Read letters to the Manager of January 21st, 24th, 26th, 29th. Read letter from Mr. Simon Harness, of the Central Union, asking for an interview with the Board. Read letter from the Men's Committee, signed David Roberts, James Green, John Bulgin, Henry Thomas, George Rous, desiring conference with the Board; and it was resolved that a special Board Meeting be called for February 7th at the house of the Manager, for the purpose of discussing the situation with Mr. Simon Harness and the Men's Committee on the spot. Passed twelve transfers, signed and sealed nine certificates and one balance certificate."
    [He pushes the book over to the CHAIRMAN.]

ANTHONY: *[With a heavy sigh.]* If it's your pleasure, sign the same.
    [He signs, moving the pen with difficulty.]

WANKLIN: What's the Union's game, Tench? They haven't made up their split with the men. What does Harness want this interview for?

TENCH: Hoping we shall come to a compromise, I think, sir; he's having a meeting with the men this afternoon.

WILDER: Harness! Ah! He's one of those cold-blooded, cool-headed chaps. I distrust them. I don't know that we didn't make a mistake to come down. What time'll the men be here?

UNDERWOOD: Any time now.

WILDER: Well, if we're not ready, they'll have to wait—won't do them any harm to cool their heels a bit.

SCANTLEBURY: *[Slowly.]* Poor devils! It's snowing. What weather!

UNDERWOOD: *[With meaning slowness.]* This house'll be the warmest place they've been in this winter.

WILDER: Well, I hope we're going to settle this business in time for me to catch the 6:30. I've got to take my wife to Spain to-morrow. *[Chattily.]* My old father had a strike at his works in '69; just such a February as this. They wanted to shoot him.

WANKLIN: What! In the close season?

WILDER: By George, there was no close season for employers then! He used to go down to his office with a pistol in his pocket.

SCANTLEBURY: *[Faintly alarmed.]* Not seriously?

WILDER: *[With finality.]* Ended in his shootin' one of 'em in the legs.

SCANTLEBURY: *[Unavoidably feeling his thigh.]* No? Which?

ANTHONY: *[Lifting the agenda paper.]* To consider the policy of the Board in relation to the strike. *[There is a silence.]*

WILDER: It's this infernal three-cornered duel—the Union, the men, and ourselves.

WANKLIN: We needn't consider the Union.

WILDER: It's my experience that you've always got to, consider the Union, confound them! If the Union were going to withdraw their support from the men, as they've done, why did they ever allow them to strike at all?

EDGAR: We've had that over a dozen times.

WILDER: Well, I've never understood it! It's beyond me. They talk of the engineers' and furnace-men's demands being excessive—so they are—but that's not enough to make the Union withdraw their support. What's behind it?

UNDERWOOD: Fear of strikes at Harper's and Tinewell's.

WILDER: *[With triumph.]* Afraid of other strikes—now, that's a reason! Why couldn't we have been told that before?

UNDERWOOD: You were.

TENCH: You were absent from the Board that day, sir.

SCANTLEBURY: The men must have seen they had no chance when the Union gave them up. It's madness.

UNDERWOOD: It's Roberts!

WILDER: Just our luck, the men finding a fanatical firebrand like Roberts for leader. *[A pause.]*

WANKLIN: *[Looking at ANTHONY.]* Well?

WILDER: *[Breaking in fussily.]* It's a regular mess. I don't like the position we're in; I don't like it; I've said so for a long time. *[Looking at WANKLIN.]* When Wanklin and I came down here before Christmas it looked as if the men must collapse. You thought so too, Underwood.

UNDERWOOD: Yes.

WILDER: Well, they haven't! Here we are, going from bad to worse losing our customers—shares going down!

SCANTLEBURY: *[Shaking his head.]* M'm! M'm!

WANKLIN: What loss have we made by this strike, Tench?

TENCH: Over fifty thousand, sir!

SCANTLEBURY: *[Pained.]* You don't say!

WILDER: We shall never got it back.

TENCH: No, sir.

WILDER: Who'd have supposed the men were going to stick out like this—nobody suggested that. *[Looking angrily at TENCH.]*

SCANTLEBURY: *[Shaking his head.]* I've never liked a fight—never shall.

ANTHONY: No surrender! *[All look at him.]*

WILDER: Who wants to surrender? *[ANTHONY looks at him.]* I—I want to act reasonably. When the men sent Roberts up to the Board in December—then was the time. We ought to have humoured him; instead of that the Chairman— [Dropping his eyes before ANTHONY'S] —er—we snapped his head off. We could have got them in then by a little tact.

ANTHONY: No compromise!

WILDER: There we are! This strike's been going on now since October, and as far as I can see it may last another six months. Pretty mess we shall be in by then. The only comfort is, the men'll be in a worse!

EDGAR: *[To UNDERWOOD.]* What sort of state are they really in, Frank?

UNDERWOOD: *[Without expression.]* Damnable!

WILDER: Well, who on earth would have thought they'd have held on like this without support!

UNDERWOOD: Those who know them.

WILDER: I defy anyone to know them! And what about tin? Price going up daily. When we do get started we shall have to work off our contracts at the top of the market.

WANKLIN: What do you say to that, Chairman?

ANTHONY: Can't be helped!

WILDER: Shan't pay a dividend till goodness knows when!

SCANTLEBURY: *[With emphasis.]* We ought to think of the shareholders. *[Turning heavily.]* Chairman, I say we ought to think of the shareholders.
        [ANTHONY mutters.]

SCANTLEBURY: What's that?

TENCH: The Chairman says he is thinking of you, sir.

SCANTLEBURY: *[Sinking back into torpor.]* Cynic!

WILDER: It's past a joke. I don't want to go without a dividend for years if the Chairman does. We can't go on playing ducks and drakes with the Company's prosperity.

EDGAR: *[Rather ashamedly.]* I think we ought to consider the men.
        [All but ANTHONY fidget in their seats.]

SCANTLEBURY: *[With a sigh.]* We mustn't think of our private feelings, young man. That'll never do.

EDGAR: *[Ironically.]* I'm not thinking of our feelings. I'm thinking of the men's.

WILDER: As to that—we're men of business.

WANKLIN: That is the little trouble.

EDGAR: There's no necessity for pushing things so far in the face of all this suffering—it's—it's cruel.
> *[No one speaks, as though EDGAR had uncovered something whose existence no man prizing his self-respect could afford to recognise.]*

WANKLIN: *[With an ironical smile.]* I'm afraid we mustn't base our policy on luxuries like sentiment.

EDGAR: I detest this state of things.

ANTHONY: We didn't seek the quarrel.

EDGAR: I know that sir, but surely we've gone far enough.

ANTHONY: No. *[All look at one another.]*

WANKLIN: Luxuries apart, Chairman, we must look out what we're doing.

ANTHONY: Give way to the men once and there'll be no end to it.

WANKLIN: I quite agree, but—
> *[ANTHONY Shakes his head]*
You make it a question of bedrock principle?
> *[ANTHONY nods.]*
Luxuries again, Chairman! The shares are below par.

WILDER: Yes, and they'll drop to a half when we pass the next dividend.

SCANTLEBURY: *[With alarm.]* Come, come! Not so bad as that.

WILDER: *[Grimly.]* You'll see*! [Craning forward to catch ANTHONY'S speech.]* I didn't catch—

TENCH: *[Hesitating.]* The Chairman says, sir, "Fais que—que—devra."

EDGAR: *[Sharply.]* My father says: "Do what we ought--and let things rip."

WILDER: Tcha!

SCANTLEBURY: *[Throwing up his hands.]* The Chairman's a Stoic—I always said the Chairman was a Stoic.

WILDER: Much good that'll do us.

WANKLIN: *[Suavely.]* Seriously, Chairman, are you going to let the ship sink under you, for the sake of—a principle?

ANTHONY: She won't sink.

SCANTLEBURY: *[With alarm.]* Not while I'm on the Board I hope.

ANTHONY: *[With a twinkle.]* Better rat, Scantlebury.

SCANTLEBURY: What a man!

ANTHONY: I've always fought them; I've never been beaten yet.

WANKLIN: We're with you in theory, Chairman. But we're not all made of cast-iron.

ANTHONY: We've only to hold on.

WILDER: *[Rising and going to the fire.]* And go to the devil as fast as we can!

ANTHONY: Better go to the devil than give in!

WILDER: *[Fretfully.]* That may suit you, sir, but it doesn't suit me, or anyone else I should think.
         [ANTHONY looks him in the face-a silence.]

EDGAR: I don't see how we can get over it that to go on like this means starvation to the men's wives and families.
> [WILDER turns abruptly to the fire, and SCANTLEBURY puts out a hand to push the idea away.]

WANKLIN: I'm afraid again that sounds a little sentimental.

EDGAR: Men of business are excused from decency, you think?

WILDER: Nobody's more sorry for the men than I am, but if they [lashing himself] choose to be such a pig-headed lot, it's nothing to do with us; we've quite enough on our hands to think of ourselves and the shareholders.

EDGAR: [Irritably.] It won't kill the shareholders to miss a dividend or two; I don't see that that's reason enough for knuckling under.

SCANTLEBURY: [With grave discomfort.] You talk very lightly of your dividends, young man; I don't know where we are.

WILDER: There's only one sound way of looking at it. We can't go on ruining ourselves with this strike.

ANTHONY: No caving in!

SCANTLEBURY: [With a gesture of despair.] Look at him!
> [ANTHONY'S leaning back in his chair. They do look at him.]

WILDER: [Returning to his seat.] Well, all I can say is, if that's the Chairman's view, I don't know what we've come down here for.

ANTHONY: To tell the men that we've got nothing for them— [Grimly.] They won't believe it till they hear it spoken in plain English.

WILDER: H'm! Shouldn't be a bit surprised if that brute Roberts hadn't got us down here with the very same idea. I hate a man with a grievance.

EDGAR: [Resentfully.] We didn't pay him enough for his discovery. I always said that at the time.

WILDER: We paid him five hundred and a bonus of two hundred three years later. If that's not enough! What does he want, for goodness' sake?

TENCH: *[Complainingly.]* Company made a hundred thousand out of his brains, and paid him seven hundred—that's the way he goes on, sir.

WILDER: The man's a rank agitator! Look here, I hate the Unions. But now we've got Harness here let's get him to settle the whole thing.

ANTHONY: No! *[Again they look at him.]*

UNDERWOOD: Roberts won't let the men assent to that.

SCANTLEBURY: Fanatic! Fanatic!

WILDER: *[Looking at ANTHONY.]* And not the only one!
        [FROST enters from the hall.]

FROST: *[To ANTHONY.]* Mr. Harness from the Union, waiting, sir. The men are here too, sir.
        [ANTHONY nods. UNDERWOOD goes to the door, returning with HARNESS, a pale, clean-shaven man with hollow cheeks, quick eyes, and lantern jaw—FROST has retired.]

UNDERWOOD: *[Pointing to TENCH'S chair.]* Sit there next the Chairman, Harness, won't you?
        [At HARNESS'S appearance, the Board have drawn together, as it were, and turned a little to him, like cattle at a dog.]

HARNESS: *[With a sharp look round, and a bow.]* Thanks! *[He sits—his accent is slightly nasal.]* Well, gentlemen, we're going to do business at last, I hope.

WILDER: Depends on what you call business, Harness. Why don't you make the men come in?

HARNESS: *[Sardonically.]* The men are far more in the right than you are. The question with us is whether we shan't begin to support them again.
        [He ignores them all, except ANTHONY, to whom he turns in speaking.]

ANTHONY: Support them if you like; we'll put in free labour and have done with it.

HARNESS: That won't do, Mr. Anthony. You can't get free labour, and you know it.

ANTHONY: We shall see that.

HARNESS: I'm quite frank with you. We were forced to withhold our support from your men because some of their demands are in excess of current rates. I expect to make them withdraw those demands to-day: if they do, take it straight from me, gentlemen, we shall back them again at once. Now, I want to see something fixed upon before I go back to-night. Can't we have done with this old-fashioned tug-of-war business? What good's it doing you? Why don't you recognise once for all that these people are men like yourselves, and want what's good for them just as you want what's good for you. *[Bitterly.]* Your motor-cars, and champagne, and eight-course dinners.

ANTHONY: If the men will come in, we'll do something for them.

HARNESS: *[Ironically.]* Is that your opinion too, sir—and yours—and yours? *[The Directors do not answer.]* Well, all I can say is: It's a kind of high and mighty aristocratic tone I thought we'd grown out of—seems I was mistaken.

ANTHONY: It's the tone the men use. Remains to be seen which can hold out longest—they without us, or we without them.

HARNESS: As business men, I wonder you're not ashamed of this waste of force, gentlemen. You know what it'll all end in.

ANTHONY: What?

HARNESS: Compromise—it always does.

SCANTLEBURY: Can't you persuade the men that their interests are the same as ours?

HARNESS: *[Turning, ironically.]* I could persuade them of that, sir, if they were.

WILDER: Come, Harness, you're a clever man, you don't believe all the Socialistic claptrap that's talked nowadays. There's no real difference between their interests and ours.

HARNESS: There's just one very simple question I'd like to put to you. Will you pay your men one penny more than they force you to pay them?
        [WILDER is silent.]

WANKLIN: *[Chiming in.]* I humbly thought that not to pay more than was necessary was the A B C of commerce.

HARNESS: *[With irony.]* Yes, that seems to be the A B C of commerce, sir; and the A B C of commerce is between your interests and the men's.

SCANTLEBURY: *[Whispering.]* We ought to arrange something.

HARNESS: *[Drily.]* Am I to understand then, gentlemen, that your Board is going to make no concessions?
        [WANKLIN and WILDER bend forward as if to speak, but stop.]

ANTHONY: *[Nodding.]* None.
        *[WANKLIN and WILDER again bend forward, and
        SCANTLEBURY gives an unexpected grunt.]*

HARNESS: You were about to say something, I believe?
        [But SCANTLEBURY says nothing.]

EDGAR: *[Looking up suddenly.]* We're sorry for the state of the men.

HARNESS: *[Icily.]* The men have no use for your pity, sir. What they want is justice.

ANTHONY: Then let them be just.

HARNESS: For that word "just" read "humble," Mr. Anthony. Why should they be humble? Barring the accident of money, aren't they as good men as you?

ANTHONY: Cant!

HARNESS: Well, I've been five years in America. It colours a man's notions.

SCANTLEBURY: *[Suddenly, as though avenging his uncompleted grunt.]* Let's have the men in and hear what they've got to say!

[ANTHONY nods, and UNDERWOOD goes out by the single door.]

HARNESS: *[Drily.]* As I'm to have an interview with them this afternoon, gentlemen, I'll ask you to postpone your final decision till that's over.
[Again ANTHONY nods, and taking up his glass drinks.]

[UNDERWOOD comes in again, followed by ROBERTS, GREEN, BULGIN, THOMAS, ROUS. They file in, hat in hand, and stand silent in a row. ROBERTS is lean, of middle height, with a slight stoop. He has a little rat-gnawn, brown-grey beard, moustaches, high cheek-bones, hollow cheeks, small fiery eyes. He wears an old and grease-stained blue serge suit, and carries an old bowler hat. He stands nearest the Chairman. GREEN, next to him, has a clean, worn face, with a small grey goatee beard and drooping moustaches, iron spectacles, and mild, straightforward eyes. He wears an overcoat, green with age, and a linen collar. Next to him is BULGIN, a tall, strong man, with a dark moustache, and fighting jaw, wearing a red muffler, who keeps changing his cap from one hand to the other. Next to him is THOMAS, an old man with a grey moustache, full beard, and weatherbeaten, bony face, whose overcoat discloses a lean, plucked-looking neck. On his right, ROUS, the youngest of the five, looks like a soldier; he has a glitter in his eyes.]

UNDERWOOD: *[Pointing.]* There are some chairs there against the wall, Roberts; won't you draw them up and sit down?

ROBERTS: Thank you, Mr. Underwood—we'll stand in the presence of the Board. *[He speaks in a biting and staccato voice, rolling his r's, pronouncing his a's like an Italian a, and his consonants short and crisp.]* How are you, Mr. Harness? Didn't expect t' have the pleasure of seeing you till this afternoon.

HARNESS: *[Steadily.]* We shall meet again then, Roberts.

ROBERTS: Glad to hear that; we shall have some news for you to take to your people.

ANTHONY: What do the men want?

ROBERTS: *[Acidly.]* Beg pardon, I don't quite catch the Chairman's remark.

TENCH: *[From behind the Chairman's chair.]* The Chairman wishes to know what the men have to say.

ROBERTS: It's what the Board has to say we've come to hear. It's for the Board to speak first.

ANTHONY: The Board has nothing to say.

ROBERTS: *[Looking along the line of men.]* In that case we're wasting the Directors' time. We'll be taking our feet off this pretty carpet.
> *[He turns, the men move slowly, as though hypnotically influenced.]*

WANKLIN: *[Suavely.]* Come, Roberts, you didn't give us this long cold journey for the pleasure of saying that.

THOMAS: *[A pure Welshman.]* No, sir, an' what I say iss—

ROBERTS: *[Bitingly.]* Go on, Henry Thomas, go on. You're better able to speak to the—Directors than me. *[THOMAS is silent.]*

TENCH: The Chairman means, Roberts, that it was the men who asked for the conference, the Board wish to hear what they have to say.

ROBERTS: Gad! If I was to begin to tell ye all they have to say, I wouldn't be finished to-day. And there'd be some that'd wish they'd never left their London palaces.

HARNESS: What's your proposition, man? Be reasonable.

ROBERTS: You want reason Mr. Harness? Take a look round this afternoon before the meeting. *[He looks at the men; no sound escapes them.]* You'll see some very pretty scenery.

HARNESS: All right my friend; you won't put me off.

ROBERTS: *[To the men.]* We shan't put Mr. Harness off. Have some champagne with your lunch, Mr. Harness; you'll want it, sir.

HARNESS: Come, get to business, man!

THOMAS: What we're asking, look you, is just simple justice.

ROBERTS: *[Venomously.]* Justice from London? What are you talking about, Henry Thomas? Have you gone silly? *[THOMAS is silent.]* We know very well what we are—discontented dogs—never satisfied. What did the Chairman tell me up in London? That I didn't know what I was talking about. I was a foolish, uneducated man, that knew nothing of the wants of the men I spoke for.

EDGAR: Do please keep to the point.

ANTHONY: *[Holding up his hand.]* There can only be one master, Roberts.

ROBERTS: Then, be Gad, it'll be us.
            [There is a silence; ANTHONY and ROBERTS stare at one
            another.]

UNDERWOOD: If you've nothing to say to the Directors, Roberts, perhaps you'll let Green or Thomas speak for the men.
            [GREEN and THOMAS look anxiously at ROBERTS, at each
            other, and the other men.]

GREEN: *[An Englishman.]* If I'd been listened to, gentlemen—

THOMAS: What I'fe got to say iss what we'fe all got to say—

ROBERTS: Speak for yourself, Henry Thomas.

SCANTLEBURY: *[With a gesture of deep spiritual discomfort.]* Let the poor men call their souls their own!

ROBERTS: Aye, they shall keep their souls, for it's not much body that you've left them, Mr. *[with biting emphasis, as though the word were an offence]* Scantlebury! *[To the men.]* Well, will you speak, or shall I speak for you?

ROUS: *[Suddenly.]* Speak out, Roberts, or leave it to others.

ROBERTS: *[Ironically.]* Thank you, George Rous. *[Addressing himself to ANTHONY.]* The Chairman and Board of Directors have honoured us by leaving London and coming all this way to hear what we've got to say; it would not be polite to keep them any longer waiting.

WILDER: Well, thank God for that!

ROBERTS: Ye will not dare to thank Him when I have done, Mr. Wilder, for all your piety. May be your God up in London has no time to listen to the working man. I'm told He is a wealthy God; but if he listens to what I tell Him, He will know more than ever He learned in Kensington.

HARNESS: Come, Roberts, you have your own God. Respect the God of other men.

ROBERTS: That's right, sir. We have another God down here; I doubt He is rather different to Mr. Wilder's. Ask Henry Thomas; he will tell you whether his God and Mr. Wilder's are the same.
> *[THOMAS lifts his hand, and cranes his head as though to prophesy.]*

WANKLIN: For goodness' sake, let 's keep to the point, Roberts.

ROBERTS: I rather think it is the point, Mr. Wanklin. If you can get the God of Capital to walk through the streets of Labour, and pay attention to what he sees, you're a brighter man than I take you for, for all that you're a Radical.

ANTHONY: Attend to me, Roberts! *[Roberts is silent.]* You are here to speak for the men, as I am here to speak for the Board.
> *[He looks slowly round. WILDER, WANKLIN, and SCANTLEBURY make movements of uneasiness, and EDGAR gazes at the floor. A faint smile comes on HARNESS'S face.]*

Now then, what is it?

ROBERTS: Right, Sir!
> *[Throughout all that follows, he and ANTHONY look fixedly upon each other. Men and Directors show in their various ways suppressed uneasiness, as though listening to words that they themselves would not have spoken.]*

The men can't afford to travel up to London; and they don't trust you to believe what they say in black and white. They know what the post is *[he darts a look at UNDERWOOD and TENCH],* and what Directors' meetings are: "Refer it to the manager—let the manager advise us on the men's condition. Can we squeeze them a little more?"

UNDERWOOD: *[In a low voice.]* Don't hit below the belt, Roberts!

ROBERTS: Is it below the belt, Mr. Underwood? The men know. When I came up to London, I told you the position straight. An' what came of it? I was told I didn't know what I was talkin' about. I can't afford to travel up to London to be told that again.

ANTHONY: What have you to say for the men?

ROBERTS: I have this to say—and first as to their condition. Ye shall 'ave no need to go and ask your manager. Ye can't squeeze them any more. Every man of us is well-nigh starving. *[A surprised murmur rises from the men. ROBERTS looks round.]* Ye wonder why I tell ye that? Every man of us is going short. We can't be no worse off than we've been these weeks past. Ye needn't think that by waiting yell drive us to come in. We'll die first, the whole lot of us. The men have sent for ye to know, once and for all, whether ye are going to grant them their demands. I see the sheet of paper in the Secretary's hand. *[TENCH moves nervously.]* That's it, I think, Mr. Tench. It's not very large.

TENCH: *[Nodding.]* Yes.

ROBERTS: There's not one sentence of writing on that paper that we can do without.
> *[A movement amongst the men. ROBERTS turns on them*
> *sharply.]*
Isn't that so?
> *[The men assent reluctantly. ANTHONY takes from TENCH the*
> *paper and peruses it.]*
Not one single sentence. All those demands are fair. We have not asked anything that we are not entitled to ask. What I said up in London, I say again now: there is not anything on that piece of paper that a just man should not ask, and a just man give.
> *[A pause.]*

ANTHONY: There is not one single demand on this paper that we will grant.

> *[In the stir that follows on these words, ROBERTS watches the Directors and ANTHONY the men. WILDER gets up abruptly and goes over to the fire.]*

ROBERTS: D' ye mean that?

ANTHONY: I do.
> *[WILDER at the fire makes an emphatic movement of disgust.]*

ROBERTS: *[Noting it, with dry intensity.]* Ye best know whether the condition of the Company is any better than the condition of the men. *[Scanning the Directors' faces.]* Ye best know whether ye can afford your tyranny—but this I tell ye: If ye think the men will give way the least part of an inch, ye're making the worst mistake ye ever made. *[He fixes his eyes on SCANTLEBURY.]* Ye think because the Union is not supporting us—more shame to it!—that we'll be coming on our knees to you one fine morning. Ye think because the men have got their wives an' families to think of—that it's just a question of a week or two—

ANTHONY: It would be better if you did not speculate so much on what we think.

ROBERTS: Aye! It's not much profit to us! I will say this for you, Mr. Anthony—ye know your own mind! *[Staring at ANTHONY.]* I can reckon on ye!

ANTHONY: *[Ironically.]* I am obliged to you!

ROBERTS: And I know mine. I tell ye this: The men will send their wives and families where the country will have to keep them; an' they will starve sooner than give way. I advise ye, Mr. Anthony, to prepare yourself for the worst that can happen to your Company. We are not so ignorant as you might suppose. We know the way the cat is jumping. Your position is not all that it might be—not exactly!

ANTHONY: Be good enough to allow us to judge of our position for ourselves. Go back, and reconsider your own.

ROBERTS: *[Stepping forward.]* Mr. Anthony, you are not a young man now; from the time I remember anything ye have been an enemy to every man that has come into your works. I don't say that ye're a mean man, or a cruel man, but ye've grudged them the say of any word in their own fate.

Ye've fought them down four times. I've heard ye say ye love a fight—mark my words—ye're fighting the last fight ye'll ever fight!
 [TENCH touches ROBERTS'S sleeve.]

UNDERWOOD: Roberts! Roberts!

ROBERTS: Roberts! Roberts! I mustn't speak my mind to the Chairman, but the Chairman may speak his mind to me!

WILDER: What are things coming to?

ANTHONY: *[With a grim smile at WILDER.]* Go on, Roberts; say what you like!

ROBERTS: *[After a pause.]* I have no more to say.

ANTHONY: The meeting stands adjourned to five o'clock.

WANKLIN: *[In a low voice to UNDERWOOD.]* We shall never settle anything like this.

ROBERTS: *[Bitingly.]* We thank the Chairman and Board of Directors for their gracious hearing.
 [He moves towards the door; the men cluster together stupefied; then ROUS, throwing up his head, passes ROBERTS and goes out. The others follow.]

ROBERTS: *[With his hand on the door--maliciously.]* Good day, gentlemen! *[He goes out.]*

HARNESS: *[Ironically.]* I congratulate you on the conciliatory spirit that's been displayed. With your permission, gentlemen, I'll be with you again at half-past five. Good morning!
 [He bows slightly, rests his eyes on ANTHONY, who returns his stare unmoved, and, followed by UNDERWOOD, goes out. There is a moment of uneasy silence. UNDERWOOD reappears in the doorway.]

WILDER: *[With emphatic disgust.]* Well!
 [The double-doors are opened.]

ENID: *[Standing in the doorway.]* Lunch is ready.

[EDGAR, getting up abruptly, walks out past his sister.]

WILDER: Coming to lunch, Scantlebury?

SCANTLEBURY: *[Rising heavily.]* I suppose so, I suppose so. It's the only thing we can do.
        [They go out through the double-doors.]

WANKLIN: *[In a low voice.]* Do you really mean to fight to a finish, Chairman?
        [ANTHONY nods.]

WANKLIN: Take care! The essence of things is to know when to stop.
        [ANTHONY does not answer.]

WANKLIN: *[Very gravely.]* This way disaster lies. The ancient Trojans were fools to your father, Mrs. Underwood. *[He goes out through the double-doors.]* I want to speak to father, Frank. *[UNDERWOOD follows WANKLIN Out. TENCH, passing round the table, is restoring order to the scattered pens and papers.]* Aren't you coming, Dad? *[ANTHONY Shakes his head. ENID looks meaningly at TENCH.]* Won't you go and have some lunch, Mr. Tench?

TENCH: *[With papers in his hand.]* Thank you, ma'am, thank you! *[He goes slowly, looking back.]*

ENID: *[Shutting the doors.]* I do hope it's settled, Father!

ANTHONY: No!

ENID: *[Very disappointed.]* Oh! Haven't you done anything!
        [ANTHONY shakes his head.]
Frank says they all want to come to a compromise, really, except that man Roberts.

ANTHONY: I don't.

ENID: It's such a horrid position for us. If you were the wife of the manager, and lived down here, and saw it all. You can't realise, Dad!

ANTHONY: Indeed?

ENID: We see all the distress. You remember my maid Annie, who married Roberts? *[ANTHONY nods.]* It's so wretched, her heart's weak; since the strike began, she hasn't even been getting proper food. I know it for a fact, Father.

ANTHONY: Give her what she wants, poor woman!

ENID: Roberts won't let her take anything from us.

ANTHONY: *[Staring before him.]* I can't be answerable for the men's obstinacy.

ENID: They're all suffering. Father! Do stop it, for my sake!

ANTHONY: *[With a keen look at her.]* You don't understand, my dear.

ENID: If I were on the Board, I'd do something.

ANTHONY: What would you do?

ENID: It's because you can't bear to give way. It's so—

ANTHONY: Well?

ENID: So unnecessary.

ANTHONY: What do you know about necessity? Read your novels, play your music, talk your talk, but don't try and tell me what's at the bottom of a struggle like this.

ENID: I live down here, and see it.

ANTHONY: What d' you imagine stands between you and your class and these men that you're so sorry for?

ENID: *[Coldly.]* I don't know what you mean, Father.

ANTHONY: In a few years you and your children would be down in the condition they're in, but for those who have the eyes to see things as they are and the backbone to stand up for themselves.

ENID: You don't know the state the men are in.

ANTHONY: I know it well enough.

ENID: You don't, Father; if you did, you wouldn't—

ANTHONY: It's you who don't know the simple facts of the position. What sort of mercy do you suppose you'd get if no one stood between you and the continual demands of labour? This sort of mercy— *[He puts his hand up to his throat and squeezes it.]* First would go your sentiments, my dear; then your culture, and your comforts would be going all the time!

ENID: I don't believe in barriers between classes.

ANTHONY: You—don't—believe—in—barriers—between the classes?

ENID: *[Coldly.]* And I don't know what that has to do with this question.

ANTHONY: It will take a generation or two for you to understand.

ENID: It's only you and Roberts, Father, and you know it!
        [ANTHONY thrusts out his lower lip.]
It'll ruin the Company.

ANTHONY: Allow me to judge of that.

ENID: *[Resentfully.]* I won't stand by and let poor Annie Roberts suffer like this! And think of the children, Father! I warn you.

ANTHONY: *[With a grim smile.]* What do you propose to do?

ENID: That's my affair.
        [ANTHONY only looks at her. She continues in a changed voice, stroking his sleeve.]
Father, you know you oughtn't to have this strain on you—you know what Dr. Fisher said!

ANTHONY: No old man can afford to listen to old women.

ENID: But you have done enough, even if it really is such a matter of principle with you.

ANTHONY: You think so?

ENID: Don't Dad! *[Her face works.]* You—you might think of us!

ANTHONY: I am.

ENID: It'll break you down.

ANTHONY: *[Slowly.]* My dear, I am not going to funk; on that you may rely.
> *[Re-enter TENCH with papers; he glances at them, then plucking up courage.]*

TENCH: Beg pardon, Madam, I think I'd rather see these papers were disposed of before I get my lunch.
> *[ENID, after an impatient glance at him, looks at her father, turns suddenly, and goes into the drawing-room. TENCH holds the papers and a pen to ANTHONY, very nervously.]*

Would you sign these for me, please sir?
> *[ANTHONY takes the pen and signs.]*

TENCH: *[Standing with a sheet of blotting-paper behind EDGAR'S chair, begins speaking nervously.]* I owe my position to you, sir.

ANTHONY: Well?

TENCH: I'm obliged to see everything that's going on, sir; I—I depend upon the Company entirely. If anything were to happen to it, it'd be disastrous for me. *[ANTHONY nods.]* And, of course, my wife's just had another; and so it makes me doubly anxious just now. And the rates are really terrible down our way.

ANTHONY: *[With grim amusement.]* Not more terrible than they are up mine.

TENCH: No, Sir? *[Very nervously.]* I know the Company means a great deal to you, sir.

ANTHONY: It does; I founded it.

TENCH: Yes, Sir. If the strike goes on it'll be very serious. I think the Directors are beginning to realise that, sir.

ANTHONY: *[Ironically.]* Indeed?

TENCH: I know you hold very strong views, sir, and it's always your habit to look things in the face; but I don't think the Directors—like it, sir, now they—they see it.

ANTHONY: *[Grimly.]* Nor you, it seems.

TENCH: *[With the ghost of a smile.]* No, sir; of course I've got my children, and my wife's delicate; in my position I have to think of these things. *[ANTHONY nods.]* It wasn't that I was going to say, sir, if you'll excuse me— *[hesitates]*

ANTHONY: Out with it, then!

TENCH: I know—from my own father, sir, that when you get on in life you do feel things dreadfully—

ANTHONY: *[Almost paternally.]* Come, out with it, Trench!

TENCH: I don't like to say it, sir.

ANTHONY: *[Stonily.]* You Must.

TENCH: *[After a pause, desperately bolting it out.]* I think the Directors are going to throw you over, sir.

ANTHONY: *[Sits in silence.]* Ring the bell!
        [TENCH nervously rings the bell and stands by the fire.]

TENCH: Excuse me for saying such a thing. I was only thinking of you, sir.
        [FROST enters from the hall, he comes to the foot of the table, and looks at ANTHONY; TENCH coveys his nervousness by arranging papers.]

ANTHONY: Bring me a whiskey and soda.

FROST: Anything to eat, sir?
        [ANTHONY shakes his head. FROST goes to the sideboard, and prepares the drink.]

TENCH: *[In a low voice, almost supplicating.]* If you could see your way, sir, it would be a great relief to my mind, it would indeed. *[He looks up at*

ANTHONY, who has not moved.] It does make me so very anxious. I
haven't slept properly for weeks, sir, and that's a fact.
           [ANTHONY looks in his face, then slowly shakes his head.]
[Disheartened.] No, Sir? [He goes on arranging papers.]
           [FROST places the whiskey and salver and puts it down by
           ANTHONY'S right hand. He stands away, looking gravely at
           ANTHONY.]

FROST: Nothing I can get you, sir? [ANTHONY shakes his head.]
You're aware, sir, of what the doctor said, sir?

ANTHONY. I am.
           [A pause. FROST suddenly moves closer to him, and speaks in a
           low voice.]

FROST: This strike, sir; puttin' all this strain on you. Excuse me, sir, is it—
is it worth it, sir?
           [ANTHONY mutters some words that are inaudible.]
Very good, sir!
           [He turns and goes out into the hall. TENCH makes two attempts
           to speak; but meeting his Chairman's gaze he drops his eyes, and,
           turning dismally, he too goes out. ANTHONY is left alone. He
           grips the glass, tilts it, and drinks deeply; then sets it down with a
           deep and rumbling sigh, and leans back in his chair.]

                         The curtain falls.

ACT II

SCENE I. The kitchen of the Roberts's cottage near the works.

*[It is half-past three. In the kitchen of Roberts's cottage a meagre
little fire is burning. The room is clean and tidy, very barely
furnished, with a brick floor and white-washed walls, much
stained with smoke. There is a kettle on the fire. A door opposite
the fireplace opens inward from a snowy street. On the wooden
table are a cup and saucer, a teapot, knife, and plate of bread and
cheese. Close to the fireplace in an old arm-chair, wrapped in a
rug, sits MRS. ROBERTS, a thin and dark-haired woman about
thirty-five, with patient eyes. Her hair is not done up, but tied
back with a piece of ribbon. By the fire, too, is MRS. YEO; a red-
haired, broad-faced person. Sitting near the table is MRS. ROUS,
an old lady, ashen-white, with silver hair; by the door, standing,
as if about to go, is MRS. BULGIN, a little pale, pinched-up
woman. In a chair, with her elbows resting on the table, avid her
face resting in her hands, sits MADGE THOMAS, a good-looking
girl, of twenty-two, with high cheekbones, deep-set eyes, and dark
untidy hair. She is listening to the talk, but she neither speaks nor
moves.]*

MRS. YEO: So he give me a sixpence, and that's the first bit o' money I seen
this week. There an't much 'eat to this fire. Come and warm yerself Mrs.
Rous, you're lookin' as white as the snow, you are.

MRS. ROUS: *[Shivering—placidly.]* Ah! but the winter my old man was
took was the proper winter. Seventy-nine that was, when none of you was
hardly born—not Madge Thomas, nor Sue Bulgin. *[Looking at them in
turn.]* Annie Roberts, 'ow old were you, dear?

MRS ROBERTS: Seven, Mrs. Rous.

MRS. ROUS: Seven—well, there! A tiny little thing!

MRS. YEO: *[Aggressively.]* Well, I was ten myself, I remembers it.

MRS. ROUS: *[Placidly.]* The Company hadn't been started three years.
Father was workin' on the acid, that's 'ow he got 'is pisoned-leg. I kep' sayin'
to 'im, "Father, you've got a pisoned leg." "Well," 'e said, "Mother, pison or

no pison, I can't afford to go a-layin' up." An' two days after, he was on 'is back, and never got up again. It was Providence! There wasn't none o' these Compensation Acts then.

MRS. YEO: Ye hadn't no strike that winter! *[With grim humour.]* This winter's 'ard enough for me. Mrs. Roberts, you don't want no 'arder winter, do you? Wouldn't seem natural to 'ave a dinner, would it, Mrs. Bulgin?

MRS. BULGIN: We've had bread and tea last four days.

MRS. YEO: You got that Friday's laundry job?

MRS. BULGIN: *[Dispiritedly.]* They said they'd give it me, but when I went last Friday, they were full up. I got to go again next week.

MRS. YEO: Ah! There's too many after that. I send Yeo out on the ice to put on the gentry's skates an' pick up what 'e can. Stops 'im from broodin' about the 'ouse.

MRS. BULGIN: *[In a desolate, matter-of-fact voice.]* Leavin' out the men—it's bad enough with the children. I keep 'em in bed, they don't get so hungry when they're not running about; but they're that restless in bed they worry your life out.

MRS. YEO: You're lucky they're all so small. It's the goin' to school that makes 'em 'ungry. Don't Bulgin give you anythin'?

MRS. BULGIN: *[Shakes her head, then, as though by afterthought.]* Would if he could, I s'pose.

MRS. YEO: *[Sardonically.]* What! 'Aven't 'e got no shares in the Company?

MRS. ROUS: *[Rising with tremulous cheerfulness.]* Well, good-bye, Annie Roberts, I'm going along home.

MRS. ROBERTS: Stay an' have a cup of tea, Mrs. Rous?

MRS. ROUS: *[With the faintest smile.]* Roberts 'll want 'is tea when he comes in. I'll just go an' get to bed; it's warmer there than anywhere.
  [She moves very shakily towards the door.]

MRS. YEO: *[Rising and giving her an arm.]* Come on, Mother, take my arm; we're all going' the same way.

MRS. ROUS: *[Taking the arm.]* Thank you, my dearies!
            [THEY go out, followed by MRS. BULGIN.]

MADGE: *[Moving for the first time.]* There, Annie, you see that! I told George Rous, "Don't think to have my company till you've made an end of all this trouble. You ought to be ashamed," I said, "with your own mother looking like a ghost, and not a stick to put on the fire. So long as you're able to fill your pipes, you'll let us starve." "I'll take my oath, Madge," he said, "I've not had smoke nor drink these three weeks!" "Well, then, why do you go on with it?" "I can't go back on Roberts!" . . . That's it! Roberts, always Roberts! They'd all drop it but for him. When he talks it's the devil that comes into them.
            [A silence. MRS. ROBERTS makes a movement of pain.]
Ah! You don't want him beaten! He's your man. With everybody like their own shadows! *[She makes a gesture towards MRS. ROBERTS.]* If Rous wants me he must give up Roberts. If he gave him up—they all would. They're only waiting for a lead. Father's against him—they're all against him in their hearts.

MRS. ROBERTS: You won't beat Roberts!
            [They look silently at each other.]

MADGE: Won't I? The cowards—when their own mothers and their own children don't know where to turn.

MRS. ROBERTS: Madge!

MADGE: *[Looking searchingly at MRS. ROBERTS.]* I wonder he can look you in the face. *[She squats before the fire, with her hands out to the flame.]* Harness is here again. They'll have to make up their minds to-day.

MRS. ROBERTS: *[In a soft, slow voice, with a slight West-country burr.]* Roberts will never give up the furnace-men and engineers. 'T wouldn't be right.

MADGE: You can't deceive me. It's just his pride.
            [A tapping at the door is heard, the women turn as ENID enters. She wears a round fur cap, and a jacket of squirrel's fur. She closes the door behind her.]

ENID: Can I come in, Annie?

MRS. ROBERTS: *[Flinching.]* Miss Enid! Give Mrs. Underwood a chair, Madge!
      [MADGE gives ENID the chair she has been sitting on.]

ENID: Thank you! *[To MRS. ROBERTS.]* Are you any better?

MRS. ROBERTS: Yes, M'm; thank you, M'm.

ENID: *[Looking at the sullen MADGE as though requesting her departure.]* Why did you send back the jelly? I call that really wicked of you!

MRS. ROBERTS: Thank you, M'm, I'd no need for it.

ENID: Of course! It was Roberts's doing, wasn't it? How can he let all this suffering go on amongst you?

MADGE: *[Suddenly.]* What suffering?

ENID: *[Surprised.]* I beg your pardon!

MADGE: Who said there was suffering?

MRS. ROBERTS: Madge!

MADGE: *[Throwing her shawl over her head.]* Please to let us keep ourselves to ourselves. We don't want you coming here and spying on us.

ENID: *[Confronting her, but without rising.]* I didn't speak to you.

MADGE: *[In a low, fierce voice.]* Keep your kind feelings to yourself. You think you can come amongst us, but you're mistaken. Go back and tell the Manager that.

ENID: *[Stonily.]* This is not your house.

MADGE: *[Turning to the door.]* No, it is not my house; keep clear of my house, Mrs. Underwood.
      [She goes out. ENID taps her fingers on the table.]

MRS. ROBERTS: Please to forgive Madge Thomas, M'm; she's a bit upset to-day.

    [A pause.]

ENID: *[Looking at her.]* Oh, I think they're so stupid, all of them.

MRS. ROBERTS: *[With a faint smile.]* Yes, M'm.

ENID: Is Roberts out?

MRS. ROBERTS: Yes, M'm.

ENID: It is his doing, that they don't come to an agreement. Now isn't it, Annie?

MRS. ROBERTS: *[Softly, with her eyes on ENID, and moving the fingers of one hand continually on her breast.]* They do say that your father, M'm—

ENID: My father's getting an old man, and you know what old men are.

MRS. ROBERTS: I am sorry, M'm.

ENID: *[More softly.]* I don't expect you to feel sorry, Annie. I know it's his fault as well as Roberts's.

MRS. ROBERTS: I'm sorry for any one that gets old, M'm; it's dreadful to get old, and Mr. Anthony was such a fine old man, I always used to think.

ENID: *[Impulsively.]* He always liked you, don't you remember? Look here, Annie, what can I do? I do so want to know. You don't get what you ought to have. *[Going to the fire, she takes the kettle off, and looks for coals.]* And you're so naughty sending back the soup and things.

MRS. ROBERTS: *[With a faint smile.]* Yes, M'm?

ENID: [Resentfully.] Why, you haven't even got coals?

MRS. ROBERTS: If you please, M'm, to put the kettle on again; Roberts won't have long for his tea when he comes in. He's got to meet the men at four.

ENID: *[Putting the kettle on.]* That means he'll lash them into a fury again. Can't you stop his going, Annie?
        [MRS. ROBERTS smiles ironically.]
Have you tried?
        [A silence.]
Does he know how ill you are?

MRS. ROBERTS: It's only my weak 'eard, M'm.

ENID: You used to be so well when you were with us.

MRS. ROBERTS: *[Stiffening.]* Roberts is always good to me.

ENID: But you ought to have everything you want, and you have nothing!

MRS. ROBERTS: *[Appealingly.]* They tell me I don't look like a dyin' woman?

ENID: Of course you don't; if you could only have proper— Will you see my doctor if I send him to you? I'm sure he'd do you good.

MRS. ROBERTS: *[With faint questioning.]* Yes, M'm.

ENID: Madge Thomas oughtn't to come here; she only excites you. As if I didn't know what suffering there is amongst the men! I do feel for them dreadfully, but you know they have gone too far.

MRS. ROBERTS: *[Continually moving her fingers.]* They say there's no other way to get better wages, M'm.

ENID: *[Earnestly.]* But, Annie, that's why the Union won't help them. My husband's very sympathetic with the men, but he says they are not underpaid.

MRS. ROBERTS: No, M'm?

ENID: They never think how the Company could go on if we paid the wages they want.

MRS. ROBERTS: *[With an effort.]* But the dividends having been so big, M'm.

ENID: *[Takes aback.]* You all seem to think the shareholders are rich men, but they're not—most of them are really no better off than working men.
        [MRS. ROBERTS smiles.]
They have to keep up appearances.

MRS. ROBERTS: Yes, M'm?

ENID: You don't have to pay rates and taxes, and a hundred other things that they do. If the men didn't spend such a lot in drink and betting they'd be quite well off!

MRS. ROBERTS: They say, workin' so hard, they must have some pleasure.

ENID: But surely not low pleasure like that.

MRS. ROBERTS: *[A little resentfully.]* Roberts never touches a drop; and he's never had a bet in his life.

ENID: Oh! but he's not a com— I mean he's an engineer—a superior man.

MRS. ROBERTS: Yes, M'm. Roberts says they've no chance of other pleasures.

ENID: *[Musing.]* Of course, I know it's hard.

MRS. ROBERTS: *[With a spice of malice.]* And they say gentlefolk's just as bad.

ENID: *[With a smile.]* I go as far as most people, Annie, but you know, yourself, that's nonsense.

MRS. ROBERTS: *[With painful effort.]* A lot 'o the men never go near the Public; but even they don't save but very little, and that goes if there's illness.

ENID: But they've got their clubs, haven't they?

MRS. ROBERTS: The clubs only give up to eighteen shillin's a week, M'm, and it's not much amongst a family. Roberts says workin' folk have always lived from hand to mouth. Sixpence to-day is worth more than a shillin' to-morrow, that's what they say.

ENID: But that's the spirit of gambling.

MRS. ROBERTS: *[With a sort of excitement.]* Roberts says a working
man's life is all a gamble, from the time 'e 's born to the time 'e dies.
> *[ENID leans forward, interested. MRS. ROBERTS goes on with a
> growing excitement that culminates in the personal feeling of the
> last words.]*

He says, M'm, that when a working man's baby is born, it's a toss-up from
breath to breath whether it ever draws another, and so on all 'is life; an' when
he comes to be old, it's the workhouse or the grave. He says that without a
man is very near, and pinches and stints 'imself and 'is children to save, there
can't be neither surplus nor security. That's why he wouldn't have no
children *[she sinks back]*, not though I wanted them.

ENID: Yes, yes, I know!

MRS. ROBERTS: No you don't, M'm. You've got your children, and you'll
never need to trouble for them.

ENID: *[Gently.]* You oughtn't to be talking so much, Annie. *[Then, in spite
of herself.]* But Roberts was paid a lot of money, wasn't he, for discovering
that process?

MRS. ROBERTS: *[On the defensive.]* All Roberts's savin's have gone. He
's always looked forward to this strike. He says he's no right to a farthing
when the others are suffering. 'T isn't so with all o' them! Some don't seem
to care no more than that—so long as they get their own.

ENID: I don't see how they can be expected to when they 're suffering like
this. *[In a changed voice.]* But Roberts ought to think of you! It's all
terrible—! The kettle's boiling. Shall I make the tea? *[She takes the teapot
and, seeing tea there, pours water into it.]* Won't you have a cup?

MRS. ROBERTS: No, thank you, M'm. *[She is listening, as though for
footsteps.]* I'd—sooner you did n't see Roberts, M'm, he gets so wild.

ENID: Oh! but I must, Annie; I'll be quite calm, I promise.

MRS. ROBERTS: It's life an' death to him, M'm.

ENID: *[Very gently.]* I'll get him to talk to me outside, we won't excite you.

MRS. ROBERTS: *[Faintly.]* No, M'm.
     [She gives a violent start. ROBERTS has come in, unseen.]

ROBERTS: *[Removing his hat—with subtle mockery.]* Beg pardon for coming in; you're engaged with a lady, I see.

ENID: Can I speak to you, Mr. Roberts?

ROBERTS: Whom have I the pleasure of addressing, Ma'am?

ENID: But surely you know me! I 'm Mrs. Underwood.

ROBERTS: *[With a bow of malice.]* The daughter of our Chairman.

ENID: *[Earnestly.]* I've come on purpose to speak to you; will you come outside a minute?
     [She looks at MRS. ROBERTS.]

ROBERTS: *[Hanging up his hat.]* I have nothing to say, Ma'am.

ENID: But I must speak to you, please.
     [She moves towards the door.]

ROBERTS: *[With sudden venom.]* I have not the time to listen!

MRS. ROBERTS: David!

ENID: Mr. Roberts, please!

ROBERTS: *[Taking off his overcoat.]* I am sorry to disoblige a lady—Mr. Anthony's daughter.

ENID: *[Wavering, then with sudden decision.]* Mr. Roberts, I know you've another meeting of the men. *[ROBERTS bows.]* I came to appeal to you. Please, please, try to come to some compromise; give way a little, if it's only for your own sakes!

ROBERTS: *[Speaking to himself.]* The daughter of Mr. Anthony begs me to give way a little, if it's only for our own sakes!

ENID: For everybody's sake; for your wife's sake.

ROBERTS: For my wife's sake, for everybody's sake—for the sake of Mr. Anthony.

ENID: Why are you so bitter against my father? He has never done anything to you.

ROBERTS: Has he not?

ENID: He can't help his views, any more than you can help yours.

ROBERTS: I really didn't know that I had a right to views!

ENID: He's an old man, and you—
          [Seeing his eyes fixed on her, she stops.]

ROBERTS: [Without raising his voice.] If I saw Mr. Anthony going to die, and I could save him by lifting my hand, I would not lift the little finger of it.

ENID: You—you— [She stops again, biting her lips.]

ROBERTS: I would not, and that's flat!

ENID: [Coldly.] You don't mean what you say, and you know it!

ROBERTS: I mean every word of it.

ENID: But why?

ROBERTS: [With a flash.] Mr. Anthony stands for tyranny! That's why!

ENID: Nonsense!
          [MRS. ROBERTS makes a movement as if to rise, but sinks back in her chair.]

ENID: [With an impetuous movement.] Annie!

ROBERTS: Please not to touch my wife!

ENID: [Recoiling with a sort of horror.] I believe—you are mad.

ROBERTS: The house of a madman then is not the fit place for a lady.

ENID: I 'm not afraid of you.

ROBERTS: *[Bowing.]* I would not expect the daughter of Mr. Anthony to be afraid. Mr. Anthony is not a coward like the rest of them.

ENID: *[Suddenly.]* I suppose you think it brave, then, to go on with the struggle.

ROBERTS: Does Mr. Anthony think it brave to fight against women and children? Mr. Anthony is a rich man, I believe; does he think it brave to fight against those who haven't a penny? Does he think it brave to set children crying with hunger, an' women shivering with cold?

ENID: *[Putting up her hand, as though warding off a blow.]* My father is acting on his principles, and you know it!

ROBERTS: And so am I!

ENID: You hate us; and you can't bear to be beaten!

ROBERTS: Neither can Mr. Anthony, for all that he may say.

ENID: At any rate you might have pity on your wife.
> *[MRS. ROBERTS who has her hand pressed to her heart, takes it away, and tries to calm her breathing.]*

ROBERTS: Madam, I have no more to say.
> *[He takes up the loaf. There is a knock at the door, and UNDERWOOD comes in. He stands looking at them, ENID turns to him, then seems undecided.]*

UNDERWOOD: Enid!

ROBERTS: *[Ironically.]* Ye were not needing to come for your wife, Mr. Underwood. We are not rowdies.

UNDERWOOD: I know that, Roberts. I hope Mrs. Roberts is better. *[ROBERTS turns away without answering.]* Come, Enid!

ENID: I make one more appeal to you, Mr. Roberts, for the sake of your wife.

ROBERTS: *[With polite malice.]* If I might advise ye, Ma'am—make it for the sake of your husband and your father.

> *[ENID, suppressing a retort, goes out. UNDERWOOD opens the door for her and follows. ROBERTS, going to the fire, holds out his hands to the dying glow.]*

How goes it, my girl? Feeling better, are you?

> *[MRS. ROBERTS smiles faintly. He brings his overcoat and wraps it round her.]*

[Looking at his watch.] Ten minutes to four! *[As though inspired.]* I've seen their faces, there's no fight in them, except for that one old robber.

MRS. ROBERTS: Won't you stop and eat, David? You've 'ad nothing all day!

ROBERTS: *[Putting his hand to his throat.]* Can't swallow till those old sharks are out o' the town: *[He walks up and down.]* I shall have a bother with the men—there's no heart in them, the cowards. Blind as bats, they are—can't see a day before their noses.

MRS. ROBERTS: It's the women, David.

ROBERTS: Ah! So they say! They can remember the women when their own bellies speak! The women never stop them from the drink; but from a little suffering to themselves in a sacred cause, the women stop them fast enough.

MRS. ROBERTS: But think o' the children, David.

ROBERTS: Ah! If they will go breeding themselves for slaves, without a thought o' the future o' them they breed—

MRS. ROBERTS: *[Gasping.]* That's enough, David; don't begin to talk of that—I won't—I can't—

ROBERTS: *[Staring at her.]* Now, now, my girl!

MRS. ROBERTS: *[Breathlessly.]* No, no, David—I won't!

ROBERTS: There, there! Come, come! That's right! *[Bitterly.]* Not one penny will they put by for a day like this. Not they! Hand to mouth—Gad!—I know them! They've broke my heart. There was no holdin' them at the start, but now the pinch 'as come.

MRS. ROBERTS: How can you expect it, David? They're not made of iron.

ROBERTS: Expect it? Wouldn't I expect what I would do meself? Wouldn't I starve an' rot rather than give in? What one man can do, another can.

MRS. ROBERTS: And the women?

ROBERTS: This is not women's work.

MRS. ROBERTS: *[With a flash of malice.]* No, the women may die for all you care. That's their work.

ROBERTS: *[Averting his eyes.]* Who talks of dying? No one will die till we have beaten these— *[He meets her eyes again, and again turns his away. Excitedly.]* This is what I've been waiting for all these months. To get the old robbers down, and send them home again without a farthin's worth o' change. I've seen their faces, I tell you, in the valley of the shadow of defeat.
              [He goes to the peg and takes down his hat.]

MRS. ROBERTS: *[Following with her eyes-softly.]* Take your overcoat, David; it must be bitter cold.

ROBERTS: *[Coming up to her-his eyes are furtive.]* No, no! There, there, stay quiet and warm. I won't be long, my girl.

MRS. ROBERTS: *[With soft bitterness.]* You'd better take it.
              [She lifts the coat. But ROBERTS puts it back, and wraps it
              round her. He tries to meet her eyes, but cannot. MRS.
              ROBERTS stays huddled in the coat, her eyes, that follow him
              about, are half malicious, half yearning. He looks at his watch
              again, and turns to go. In the doorway he meets JAN THOMAS, a
              boy of ten in clothes too big for him, carrying a penny whistle.]

ROBERTS: Hallo, boy!
              [He goes. JAN stops within a yard of MRS. ROBERTS, and stares
              at her without a word.]

MRS. ROBERTS: Well, Jan!

JAN: Father 's coming; sister Madge is coming.

[He sits at the table, and fidgets with his whistle; he blows three vague notes; then imitates a cuckoo.]

[There is a tap on the door. Old THOMAS comes in.]

THOMAS: A very coot tay to you, Ma'am. It is petter that you are.

MRS. ROBERTS: Thank you, Mr. Thomas.

THOMAS: *[Nervously.]* Roberts in?

MRS. ROBERTS: Just gone on to the meeting, Mr. Thomas.

THOMAS: *[With relief, becoming talkative.]* This is fery unfortunate, look you! I came to tell him that we must make terms with London. It is a fery great pity he is gone to the meeting. He will be kicking against the pricks, I am thinking.

MRS. ROBERTS: *[Half rising.]* He'll never give in, Mr. Thomas.

THOMAS: You must not be fretting, that is very pat for you. Look you, there iss hartly any mans for supporting him now, but the engineers and George Rous. *[Solemnly.]* This strike is no longer Going with Chapel, look you! I have listened carefully, an' I have talked with her. *[JAN blows.]* Sst! I don't care what th' others say, I say that Chapel means us to be stopping the trouple, that is what I make of her; and it is my opinion that this is the fery best thing for all of us. If it wasn't my opinion, I ton't say but it is my opinion, look you.

MRS. ROBERTS: *[Trying to suppress her excitement.]* I don't know what'll come to Roberts, if you give in.

THOMAS: It iss no disgrace whateffer! All that a mortal man coult do he hass tone. It iss against Human Nature he hass gone; fery natural any man may do that; but Chapel has spoken and he must not go against her. *[JAN imitates the cuckoo.]* Ton't make that squeaking! *[Going to the door.]* Here Iss my daughter come to sit with you. A fery goot day, Ma'am—no fretting—rememper!
        [MADGE comes in and stands at the open door, watching the street.]

MADGE: You'll be late, Father; they're beginning. *[She catches him by the sleeve.]* For the love of God, stand up to him, Father—this time!

THOMAS: *[Detaching his sleeve with dignity.]* Leave me to do what's proper, girl!
> *[He goes out. MADGE, in the centre of the open doorway, slowly moves in, as though before the approach of someone.]*

ROUS: *[Appearing in the doorway.]* Madge!
> *[MADGE stands with her back to MRS. ROBERTS, staring at him with her head up and her hands behind her.]*

ROUS: *[Who has a fierce distracted look.]* Madge! I'm going to the meeting. *[MADGE, without moving, smiles contemptuously.]* D' ye hear me?
> *[They speak in quick low voices.]*

MADGE: I hear! Go, and kill your own mother, if you must.
> *[ROUS seizes her by both her arms. She stands rigid, with her head bent back. He releases her, and he too stands motionless.]*

ROUS: I swore to stand by Roberts. I swore that! Ye want me to go back on what I've sworn.

MADGE: *[With slow soft mockery.]* You are a pretty lover!

ROUS: Madge!

MADGE: *[Smiling.]* I've heard that lovers do what their girls ask them— *[JAN sounds the cuckoo's notes]* —but that's not true, it seems!

ROUS: You'd make a blackleg of me!

MADGE: *[With her eyes half-closed.]* Do it for me!

ROUS: *[Dashing his hand across his brow.]* Damn! I can't!

MADGE: *[Swiftly.]* Do it for me!

ROUS: *[Through his teeth.]* Don't play the wanton with me!

MADGE: *[With a movement of her hand towards JAN—quick and low.]*
I would be that for the children's sake!

ROUS: *[In a fierce whisper.]* Madge! Oh, Madge!

MADGE: *[With soft mockery.]* But you can't break your word for me!

ROUS: *[With a choke.]* Then, Begod, I can!
    [He turns and rushes off.]

    [MADGE Stands, with a faint smile on her face, looking after
    him. She turns to MRS. ROBERTS.]

MADGE: I have done for Roberts!

MRS. ROBERTS: *[Scornfully.]* Done for my man, with that—!
    [She sinks back.]

MADGE: *[Running to her, and feeling her hands.]* You're as cold as a
stone! You want a drop of brandy. Jan, run to the "Lion"; say, I sent you
for Mrs. Roberts.

MRS. ROBERTS: *[With a feeble movement.]* I'll just sit quiet, Madge.
Give Jan—his—tea.

MADGE: *[Giving JAN a slice of bread.]* There, ye little rascal. Hold your
piping. *[Going to the fire, she kneels.]* It's going out.

MRS. ROBERTS: *[With a faint smile.]* 'T is all the same!
    [JAN begins to blow his whistle.]

MADGE: Tsht! Tsht!—you
    [JAN Stops.]

MRS. ROBERTS: *[Smiling.]* Let 'im play, Madge.

MADGE: *[On her knees at the fire, listening.]* Waiting an' waiting. I've no
patience with it; waiting an' waiting—that's what a woman has to do! Can
you hear them at it—I can!

[*JAN begins again to play his whistle; MADGE gets up; half tenderly she ruffles his hair; then, sitting, leans her elbows on the table, and her chin on her hands. Behind her, on MRS. ROBERTS'S face the smile has changed to horrified surprise. She makes a sudden movement, sitting forward, pressing her hands against her breast. Then slowly she sinks' back; slowly her face loses the look of pain, the smile returns. She fixes her eyes again on JAN, and moves her lips and finger to the tune.*]

The curtain falls.

SCENE II. A space outside the works.

[It is past four. In a grey, failing light, an open muddy space is crowded with workmen. Beyond, divided from it by a barbed-wire fence, is the raised towing-path of a canal, on which is moored a barge. In the distance are marshes and snow-covered hills. The "Works" high wall runs from the canal across the open space, and in the angle of this wall is a rude platform of barrels and boards. On it, HARNESS is standing. ROBERTS, a little apart from the crowd, leans his back against the wall. On the raised towing-path two bargemen lounge and smoke indifferently.]

HARNESS: *[Holding out his hand.]* Well, I've spoken to you straight. If I speak till to-morrow I can't say more.

JAGO: *[A dark, sallow, Spanish-looking man with a short, thin beard.]* Mister, want to ask you! Can they get blacklegs?

BULGIN: *[Menacing.]* Let 'em try.
          [There are savage murmurs from the crowd.]

BROWN: *[A round-faced man.]* Where could they get 'em then?

EVANS: *[A small, restless, harassed man, with a fighting face.]* There's always blacklegs; it's the nature of 'em. There's always men that'll save their own skins.
          [Another savage murmur. There is a movement, and old THOMAS, joining the crowd, takes his stand in front.]

HARNESS: *[Holding up his hand.]* They can't get them. But that won't help you. Now men, be reasonable. Your demands would have brought on us the burden of a dozen strikes at a time when we were not prepared for them. The Unions live by justice, not to one, but all. Any fair man will tell you—you were ill-advised! I don't say you go too far for that which you're entitled to, but you're going too far for the moment; you've dug a pit for yourselves. Are you to stay there, or are you to climb out? Come!

LEWIS: *[A clean-cut Welshman with a dark moustache.]* You've hit it, Mister! Which is it to be?
          [Another movement in the crowd, and ROUS, coming quickly, takes his stand next THOMAS.]

HARNESS: Cut your demands to the right pattern, and we'll see you through; refuse, and don't expect me to waste my time coming down here again. I'm not the sort that speaks at random, as you ought to know by this time. If you're the sound men I take you for—no matter who advises you against it— *[he fixes his eyes on ROBERTS]* you'll make up your minds to come in, and trust to us to get your terms. Which is it to be? Hands together, and victory—or—the starvation you've got now?
> *[A prolonged murmur from the crowd.]*

JAGO: *[Sullenly.]* Talk about what you know.

HARNESS: *[Lifting his voice above the murmur.]* Know? *[With cold passion.]* All that you've been through, my friend, I've been through—I was through it when I was no bigger than *[pointing to a youth]* that shaver there; the Unions then weren't what they are now. What's made them strong? It's hands together that's made them strong. I've been through it all, I tell you, the brand's on my soul yet. I know what you've suffered—there's nothing you can tell me that I don't know; but the whole is greater than the part, and you are only the part. Stand by us, and we will stand by you.
> *[Quartering them with his eyes, he waits. The murmuring swells; the men form little groups. GREEN, BULGIN, and LEWIS talk together.]*

LEWIS: Speaks very sensible, the Union chap.

GREEN: *[Quietly.]* Ah! if I 'd a been listened to, you'd 'ave 'eard sense these two months past.
> *[The bargemen are seen laughing.]*

LEWIS: *[Pointing.]* Look at those two blanks over the fence there!

BULGIN: *[With gloomy violence.]* They'd best stop their cackle, or I'll break their jaws.

JAGO: *[Suddenly.]* You say the furnace men's paid enough?

HARNESS: I did not say they were paid enough; I said they were paid as much as the furnace men in similar works elsewhere.

EVANS: That's a lie! *[Hubbub.]* What about Harper's?

HARNESS: *[With cold irony.]* You may look at home for lies, my man. Harper's shifts are longer, the pay works out the same.

HENRY ROUS: *[A dark edition of his brother George.]* Will ye support us in double pay overtime Saturdays?

HARNESS: Yes, we will.

JAGO: What have ye done with our subscriptions?

HARNESS: *[Coldly.]* I have told you what we will do with them.

EVANS: Ah! will, it's always will! Ye'd have our mates desert us.
        [Hubbub.]

BULGIN: *[Shouting.]* Hold your row!
        [EVANS looks round angrily.]

HARNESS: *[Lifting his voice.]* Those who know their right hands from their lefts know that the Unions are neither thieves nor traitors. I've said my say. Figure it out, my lads; when you want me you know where I shall be.
        [He jumps down, the crowd gives way, he passes through them, and goes away. A BARGEMAN looks after him jerking his pipe with a derisive gesture. The men close up in groups, and many looks are cast at ROBERTS, who stands alone against the wall.]

EVANS: He wants ye to turn blacklegs, that's what he wants. He wants ye to go back on us. Sooner than turn blackleg—I 'd starve, I would.

BULGIN: Who's talkin' o' blacklegs—mind what you're saying, will you?

BLACKSMITH: *[A youth with yellow hair and huge arms.]* What about the women?

EVANS: They can stand what we can stand, I suppose, can't they?

BLACKSMITH: Ye've no wife?

EVANS: An' don't want one!

THOMAS: *[Raising his voice.]* Aye! Give us the power to come to terms with London, lads.

DAVIES: *[A dark, slow-fly, gloomy man.]* Go up the platform, if you got anything to say, go up an' say it.
> *[There are cries of "Thomas!" He is pushed towards the platform; he ascends it with difficulty, and bares his head, waiting for silence. A hush.]*

RED-HAIRED YOUTH: *[suddenly.]* Coot old Thomas!
> *[A hoarse laugh; the bargemen exchange remarks; a hush again, and THOMAS begins speaking.]*

THOMAS: We are all in the tepth together, and it iss Nature that has put us there.

HENRY ROUS: It's London put us there!

EVANS: It's the Union.

THOMAS: It iss not Lonton; nor it iss not the Union—it iss Nature. It iss no disgrace whateffer to a potty to give in to Nature. For this Nature iss a fery pig thing; it is pigger than what a man is. There iss more years to my hett than to the hett of any one here. It is fery pat, look you, this Going against Nature. It is pat to make other potties suffer, when there is nothing to pe cot py it.
> *[A laugh. THOMAS angrily goes on.]*
What are ye laughing at? It is pat, I say! We are fighting for a principle; there is no potty that shall say I am not a peliever in principle. Putt when Nature says "No further," then it is no coot snapping your fingers in her face.
> *[A laugh from ROBERTS, and murmurs of approval.]*
This Nature must pe humort. It is a man's pisiness to pe pure, honest, just, and merciful. That's what Chapel tells you. *[To ROBERTS, angrily.]* And, look you, David Roberts, Chapel tells you ye can do that without Going against Nature.

JAGO: What about the Union?

THOMAS: I ton't trust the Union; they haf treated us like tirt. "Do what we tell you," said they. I haf peen captain of the furnace-men twenty years, and I say to the Union— *[excitedly]* —"Can you tell me then, as well as I can tell you, what iss the right wages for the work that these men do?" For fife and twenty years I haf paid my moneys to the Union and— *[with great excitement]* —for nothings! What iss that but roguery, for all that this Mr. Harness says!

EVANS: Hear, hear.

HENRY ROUS: Get on with you! Cut on with it then!

THOMAS: Look you, if a man toes not trust me, am I going to trust him?

JAGO: That's right.

THOMAS: Let them alone for rogues, and act for ourselves.
        [Murmurs.]

BLACKSMITH: That's what we been doin', haven't we?

THOMAS: *[With increased excitement.]* I wass brought up to do for meself. I wass brought up to go without a thing, if I hat not moneys to puy it. There iss too much, look you, of doing things with other people's moneys. We haf fought fair, and if we haf peen beaten, it iss no fault of ours. Gif us the power to make terms with London for ourself; if we ton't succeed, I say it iss petter to take our peating like men, than to tie like togs, or hang on to others' coat-tails to make them do our pisiness for us!

EVANS: *[Muttering.]* Who wants to?

THOMAS: *[Craning.]* What's that? If I stand up to a potty, and he knocks me town, I am not to go hollering to other potties to help me; I am to stand up again; and if he knocks me town properly, I am to stay there, isn't that right?
        [Laughter.]

JAGO: No Union!

HENRY ROUS: Union!
        [Murmurs. Others take up the shout.]

EVANS: Blacklegs!
        [BULGIN and the BLACKSMITH shake their fists at EVANS.]

THOMAS: *[With a gesture.]* I am an olt man, look you.
        [A sudden silence, then murmurs again.]

LEWIS: Olt fool, with his "No Union!"

BULGIN: Them furnace chaps! For twopence I'd smash the faces o' the lot of them.

GREEN: If I'd a been listened to at the first!

THOMAS: *[Wiping his brow.]* I'm comin' now to what I was going to Say—

DAVIES: *[Muttering.]* An' time too!

THOMAS: *[Solemnly.]* Chapel says: Ton't carry on this strife! Put an end to it!

JAGO: That's a lie! Chapel says go on!

THOMAS: *[Scornfully.]* Inteet! I haf ears to my head.

RED-HAIRED YOUTH: Ah! long ones!
          [A laugh.]

JAGO: Your ears have misbeled you then.

THOMAS: *[Excitedly.]* Ye cannot be right if I am, ye cannot haf it both ways.

RED-HAIRED YOUTH: Chapel can though!
          ["The Shaver" laughs; there are murmurs from the crowd.]

THOMAS: *[Fixing his eyes on "The Shaver."]* Ah! ye 're Going the roat to tamnation. An' so I say to all of you. If ye co against Chapel I will not pe with you, nor will any other Got-fearing man.
          [He steps down from the platform. JAGO makes his way towards it. There are cries of "Don't let 'im go up!"]

JAGO: Don't let him go up? That's free speech, that is. *[He goes up.]* I ain't got much to say to you. Look at the matter plain; ye've come the road this far, and now you want to chuck the journey. We've all been in one boat; and now you want to pull in two. We engineers have stood by you; ye're ready now, are ye, to give us the go-by? If we'd aknown that before, we'd not a-started out with you so early one bright morning! That's all I 've got to

say. Old man Thomas a'n't got his Bible lesson right. If you give up to
London, or to Harness, now, it's givin' us the chuck—to save your skins—
you won't get over that, my boys; it's a dirty thing to do.

> *[He gets down; during his little speech, which is ironically
> spoken, there is a restless discomfort in the crowd. ROUS,
> stepping forward, jumps on the platform. He has an air of fierce
> distraction. Sullen murmurs of disapproval from the crowd.]*

ROUS: *[Speaking with great excitement.]* I'm no blanky orator, mates, but
wot I say is drove from me. What I say is yuman nature. Can a man set an'
see 'is mother starve? Can 'e now?

ROBERTS: *[Starting forward.]* Rous!

ROUS: *[Staring at him fiercely.]* Sim 'Arness said fair! I've changed my
mind!

ROBERTS: Ah! Turned your coat you mean!

> *[The crowd manifests a great surprise.]*

LEWIS: *[Apostrophising Rous.]* Hallo! What's turned him round?

ROUS: *[Speaking with intense excitement.]* 'E said fair. "Stand by us," 'e
said, "and we'll stand by you." That's where we've been makin' our mistake
this long time past; and who's to blame fort? *[He points at ROBERTS]* That
man there! "No," 'e said, "fight the robbers," 'e said, "squeeze the breath out
o' them!" But it's not the breath out o' them that's being squeezed; it's the
breath out of us and ours, and that's the book of truth. I'm no orator, mates,
it's the flesh and blood in me that's speakin', it's the heart o' me. *[With a
menacing, yet half-ashamed movement towards ROBERTS.]* He'll speak to
you again, mark my words, but don't ye listen. *[The crowd groans.]* It's
hell fire that's on that man's tongue. *[ROBERTS is seen laughing.]* Sim
'Arness is right. What are we without the Union—handful o' parched
leaves—a puff o' smoke. I'm no orator, but I say: Chuck it up! Chuck it up!
Sooner than go on starving the women and the children.

> *[The murmurs of acquiescence almost drown the murmurs of
> dissent.]*

EVANS: What's turned you to blacklegging?

ROUS: *[With a furious look.]* Sim 'Arness knows what he's talking about. Give us power to come to terms with London; I'm no orator, but I say—have done wi' this black misery!

> *[He gives his muffler a twist, jerks his head back, and jumps off the platform. The crowd applauds and surges forward. Amid cries of "That's enough!" "Up Union!" "Up Harness!" ROBERTS quietly ascends the platform. There is a moment of silence.]*

BLACKSMITH: We don't want to hear you. Shut it!

HENRY ROUS: Get down!

> *[Amid such cries they surge towards the platform.]*

EVANS: *[Fiercely.]* Let 'im speak! Roberts! Roberts!

BULGIN: *[Muttering.]* He'd better look out that I don't crack his skull.

> *[ROBERTS faces the crowd, probing them with his eyes till they gradually become silent. He begins speaking. One of the bargemen rises and stands.]*

ROBERTS: You don't want to hear me, then? You'll listen to Rous and to that old man, but not to me. You'll listen to Sim Harness of the Union that's treated you so fair; maybe you'll listen to those men from London? Ah! You groan! What for? You love their feet on your necks, don't you? *[Then as BULGIN elbows his way towards the platform, with calm pathos.]* You'd like to break my jaw, John Bulgin. Let me speak, then do your smashing, if it gives you pleasure. *[BULGIN Stands motionless and sullen.]* Am I a liar, a coward, a traitor? If only I were, ye'd listen to me, I'm sure. *[The murmurings cease, and there is now dead silence.]* Is there a man of you here that has less to gain by striking? Is there a man of you that had more to lose? Is there a man of you that has given up eight hundred pounds since this trouble here began? Come now, is there? How much has Thomas given up—ten pounds or five, or what? You listened to him, and what had he to say? "None can pretend," he said, "that I'm not a believer in principle— *[with biting irony]* —but when Nature says: 'No further, 't es going agenst Nature.'" I tell you if a man cannot say to Nature: "Budge me from this if ye can!"— *[with a sort of exaltation]* his principles are but his belly. "Oh, but," Thomas says, "a man can be pure and honest, just and merciful, and take off his hat to Nature!" I tell you Nature's neither pure nor honest, just nor merciful. You chaps that live over the hill, an' go home dead beat in the dark on a snowy night—don't ye fight your way every inch of it? Do ye go

lyin' down an' trustin' to the tender mercies of this merciful Nature? Try it
and you'll soon know with what ye've got to deal. 'T es only by that— *[he
strikes a blow with his clenched fist]* —in Nature's face that a man can be a
man. "Give in," says Thomas, "go down on your knees; throw up your
foolish fight, an' perhaps," he said, "perhaps your enemy will chuck you
down a crust."

JAGO: Never!

EVANS: Curse them!

THOMAS: I nefer said that.

ROBERTS: *[Bitingly.]* If ye did not say it, man, ye meant it. An' what did
ye say about Chapel? "Chapel's against it," ye said. "She 's against it!"
Well, if Chapel and Nature go hand in hand, it's the first I've ever heard of it.
That young man there— *[pointing to ROUS]* —said I 'ad 'ell fire on my
tongue. If I had I would use it all to scorch and wither this talking of
surrender. Surrendering's the work of cowards and traitors.

HENRY ROUS: *[As GEORGE ROUS moves forward.]* Go for him,
George—don't stand his lip!

ROBERTS: *[Flinging out his finger.]* Stop there, George Rous, it's no time
this to settle personal matters. *[ROUS stops.]* But there was one other
spoke to you—Mr. Simon Harness. We have not much to thank Mr.
Harness and the Union for. They said to us "Desert your mates, or we'll
desert you." An' they did desert us.

EVANS: They did.

ROBERTS: Mr. Simon Harness is a clever man, but he has come too late.
[With intense conviction.] For all that Mr. Simon Harness says, for all that
Thomas, Rous, for all that any man present here can say—We've won the
fight!
        [The crowd sags nearer, looking eagerly up.]
[With withering scorn.] You've felt the pinch o't in your bellies. You've
forgotten what that fight 'as been; many times I have told you; I will tell you
now this once again. The fight o' the country's body and blood against a
blood-sucker. The fight of those that spend themselves with every blow
they strike and every breath they draw, against a thing that fattens on them,
and grows and grows by the law of merciful Nature. That thing is Capital!

A thing that buys the sweat o' men's brows, and the tortures o' their brains, at its own price. Don't I know that? Wasn't the work o' my brains bought for seven hundred pounds, and hasn't one hundred thousand pounds been gained them by that seven hundred without the stirring of a finger. It is a thing that will take as much and give you as little as it can. That's Capital! A thing that will say—"I'm very sorry for you, poor fellows—you have a cruel time of it, I know," but will not give one sixpence of its dividends to help you have a better time. That's Capital! Tell me, for all their talk, is there one of them that will consent to another penny on the Income Tax to help the poor? That's Capital! A white-faced, stony-hearted monster! Ye have got it on its knees; are ye to give up at the last minute to save your miserable bodies pain? When I went this morning to those old men from London, I looked into their very 'earts. One of them was sitting there—Mr. Scantlebury, a mass of flesh nourished on us: sittin' there for all the world like the shareholders in this Company, that sit not moving tongue nor finger, takin' dividends a great dumb ox that can only be roused when its food is threatened. I looked into his eyes and I saw he was afraid—afraid for himself and his dividends; afraid for his fees, afraid of the very shareholders he stands for; and all but one of them's afraid—like children that get into a wood at night, and start at every rustle of the leaves. I ask you, men— *[he pauses, holding out his hand till there is utter silence]* — give me a free hand to tell them: "Go you back to London. The men have nothing for you!" *[A murmuring.]* Give me that, an' I swear to you, within a week you shall have from London all you want.

EVANS, JAGO, and OTHERS: A free hand! Give him a free hand! Bravo—bravo!

ROBERTS: 'T is not for this little moment of time we're fighting *[the murmuring dies]*, not for ourselves, our own little bodies, and their wants, 't is for all those that come after throughout all time. *[With intense sadness.]* Oh! Men—for the love o' them, don't roll up another stone upon their heads, don't help to blacken the sky, an' let the bitter sea in over them. They're welcome to the worst that can happen to me, to the worst that can happen to us all, aren't they—aren't they? If we can shake *[passionately]* that white-faced monster with the bloody lips, that has sucked the life out of ourselves, our wives, and children, since the world began. *[Dropping the note of passion but with the utmost weight and intensity.]* If we have not the hearts of men to stand against it breast to breast, and eye to eye, and force it backward till it cry for mercy, it will go on sucking life; and we shall stay forever what we are *[in almost a whisper]*, less than the very dogs.

*[An utter stillness, and ROBERTS stands rocking his body
slightly, with his eyes burning the faces of the crowd.]*

EVANS and JAGO: *[Suddenly.]* Roberts! *[The shout is taken up.]*
*[There is a slight movement in the crowd, and MADGE passing
below the towing-path, stops by the platform, looking up at
ROBERTS. A sudden doubting silence.]*

ROBERTS: "Nature," says that old man, "give in to Nature." I tell you,
strike your blow in Nature's face—an' let it do its worst!
[He catches sight of MADGE, his brows contract, he looks away.]

MADGE: *[In a low voice-close to the platform.]* Your wife's dying!
*[ROBERTS glares at her as if torn from some pinnacle of
exaltation.]*

ROBERTS: *[Trying to stammer on.]* I say to you—answer them—answer
Them—
[He is drowned by the murmur in the crowd.]

THOMAS: *[Stepping forward.]* Ton't you hear her, then?

ROBERTS: What is it? *[A dead silence.]*

THOMAS: Your wife, man!
*[ROBERTS hesitates, then with a gesture, he leaps down, and
goes away below the towing-path, the men making way for him.
The standing bargeman opens and prepares to light a lantern.
Daylight is fast failing.]*

MADGE: He needn't have hurried! Annie Roberts is dead. *[Then in the
silence, passionately.]* You pack of blinded hounds! How many more
women are you going to let to die?
*[The crowd shrinks back from her, and breaks up in groups, with
a confused, uneasy movement. MADGE goes quickly away below
the towing-path. There is a hush as they look after her.]*

LEWIS: There's a spitfire, for ye!

BULGIN: *[Growling.]* I'll smash 'er jaw.

GREEN: If I'd a-been listened to, that poor woman—

THOMAS: It's a judgment on him for going against Chapel. I tolt him how 't would be!

EVANS: All the more reason for sticking by 'im. *[A cheer.]* Are you goin' to desert him now 'e 's down? Are you going to chuck him over, now 'e 's lost 'is wife?
> *[The crowd is murmuring and cheering all at once.]*

ROUS: *[Stepping in front of platform.]* Lost his wife! Aye! Can't ye see? Look at home, look at your own wives! What's to save them? Ye'll have the same in all your houses before long!

LEWIS: Aye, aye!

HENRY ROUS: Right! George, right!
> *[There are murmurs of assent.]*

ROUS: It's not us that's blind, it's Roberts. How long will ye put up with 'im!

HENRY, ROUS, BULGIN, DAVIES: Give 'im the chuck!
> *[The cry is taken up.]*

EVANS: *[Fiercely.]* Kick a man that's down? Down?

HENRY ROUS: Stop his jaw there!
> *[EVANS throws up his arm at a threat from BULGIN. The bargeman, who has lighted the lantern, holds it high above his head.]*

ROUS: *[Springing on to the platform.]* What brought him down then, but 'is own black obstinacy? Are ye goin' to follow a man that can't see better than that where he's goin'?

EVANS: He's lost 'is wife.

ROUS: An' who's fault's that but his own. 'Ave done with 'im, I say, before he's killed your own wives and mothers.

DAVIES: Down 'im!

HENRY ROUS: He's finished!

BROWN: We've had enough of 'im!

BLACKSMITH: Too much!
> *[The crowd takes up these cries, excepting only EVANS, JAGO, and GREEN, who is seen to argue mildly with the BLACKSMITH.]*

ROUS: *[Above the hubbub.]* We'll make terms with the Union, lads.
> *[Cheers.]*

EVANS: *[Fiercely.]* Ye blacklegs!

BULGIN: *[Savagely-squaring up to him.]* Who are ye callin' blacklegs, Rat?
> *[EVANS throws up his fists, parries the blow, and returns it. They fight. The bargemen are seen holding up the lantern and enjoying the sight. Old THOMAS steps forward and holds out his hands.]*

THOMAS: Shame on your strife!
> *[The BLACKSMITH, BROWN, LEWIS, and the RED-HAIRED YOUTH pull EVANS and BULGIN apart. The stage is almost dark.]*

The curtain falls.

ACT III. The drawing-room of the Manager's house.

[It is five o'clock. In the UNDERWOODS' drawing-room, which is artistically furnished, ENID is sitting on the sofa working at a baby's frock. EDGAR, by a little spindle-legged table in the centre of the room, is fingering a china-box. His eyes are fixed on the double-doors that lead into the dining-room.]

EDGAR: *[Putting down the china-box, and glancing at his watch.]* Just on five, they're all in there waiting, except Frank. Where's he?

ENID: He's had to go down to Gasgoyne's about a contract. Will you want him?

EDGAR: He can't help us. This is a director's job. *[Motioning towards a single door half hidden by a curtain.]* Father in his room?

ENID: Yes.

EDGAR: I wish he'd stay there, Enid. *[ENID looks up at him.]* This is a beastly business, old girl?
         [He takes up the little box again and turns it over and over.]

ENID: I went to the Roberts's this afternoon, Ted.

EDGAR: That wasn't very wise.

ENID: He's simply killing his wife.

EDGAR: We are you mean.

ENID: *[Suddenly.]* Roberts ought to give way!

EDGAR: There's a lot to be said on the men's side.

ENID: I don't feel half so sympathetic with them as I did before I went. They just set up class feeling against you. Poor Annie was looking dread fully bad—fire going out, and nothing fit for her to eat. *[EDGAR walks to and fro.]* But she would stand up for Roberts. When you see all this wretchedness going on and feel you can do nothing, you have to shut your eyes to the whole thing.

EDGAR: If you can.

ENID: When I went I was all on their side, but as soon as I got there I began to feel quite different at once. People talk about sympathy with the working classes, they don't know what it means to try and put it into practice. It seems hopeless.

EDGAR: Ah! well.

ENID: It's dreadful going on with the men in this state. I do hope Dad will make concessions.

EDGAR: He won't. *[Gloomily.]* It's a sort of religion with him. Curse it! I know what's coming! He'll be voted down.

ENID: They wouldn't dare!

EDGAR: They will—they're in a funk.

ENID: *[Indignantly.]* He'd never stand it!

EDGAR: *[With a shrug.]* My dear girl, if you're beaten in a vote, you've got to stand it.

ENID: Oh! *[She gets up in alarm.]* But would he resign?

EDGAR: Of course! It goes to the roots of his beliefs.

ENID: But he's so wrapped up in this company, Ted! There'd be nothing left for him! It'd be dreadful! *[EDGAR shrugs his shoulders.]* Oh, Ted, he's so old now! You mustn't let them!

EDGAR: *[Hiding his feelings in an outburst.]* My sympathies in this strike are all on the side of the men.

ENID: He's been Chairman for more than thirty years! He made the whole thing! And think of the bad times they've had; it's always been he who pulled them through. Oh, Ted, you must!

EDGAR: What is it you want? You said just now you hoped he'd make concessions. Now you want me to back him in not making them. This isn't a game, Enid!

ENID: *[Hotly.]* It isn't a game to me that Dad's in danger of losing all he cares about in life. If he won't give way, and he's beaten, it'll simply break him down!

EDGAR: Didn't you say it was dreadful going on with the men in this state?

ENID: But can't you see, Ted, Father'll never get over it! You must stop them somehow. The others are afraid of him. If you back him up—

EDGAR: *[Putting his hand to his head.]* Against my convictions—against yours! The moment it begins to pinch one personally—

ENID: It isn't personal, it's Dad!

EDGAR: Your family or yourself, and over goes the show!

ENID: *[Resentfully.]* If you don't take it seriously, I do.

EDGAR: I am as fond of him as you are; that's nothing to do with it.

ENID: We can't tell about the men; it's all guess-work. But we know Dad might have a stroke any day. D' you mean to say that he isn't more to you than—

EDGAR: Of course he is.

ENID: I don't understand you then.

EDGAR: H'm!

ENID: If it were for oneself it would be different, but for our own Father! You don't seem to realise.

EDGAR: I realise perfectly.

ENID: It's your first duty to save him.

EDGAR: I wonder.

ENID: *[Imploring.]* Oh, Ted? It's the only interest he's got left; it'll be like a death-blow to him!

EDGAR: *[Restraining his emotion.]* I know.

ENID: Promise!

EDGAR: I'll do what I can.
> *[He turns to the double-doors.]*

> *[The curtained door is opened, and ANTHONY appears. EDGAR opens the double-doors, and passes through.]*

> *[SCANTLEBURY'S voice is faintly heard: "Past five; we shall never get through—have to eat another dinner at that hotel!" The doors are shut. ANTHONY walks forward.]*

ANTHONY: You've been seeing Roberts, I hear.

ENID: Yes.

ANTHONY: Do you know what trying to bridge such a gulf as this is like?
> *[ENID puts her work on the little table, and faces him.]*
Filling a sieve with sand!

ENID: Don't!

ANTHONY: You think with your gloved hands you can cure the trouble of the century.
> *[He passes on.]*

ENID: Father!
> *[ANTHONY Stops at the double doors.]*
I'm only thinking of you!

ANTHONY: *[More softly.]* I can take care of myself, my dear.

ENID: Have you thought what'll happen if you're beaten— *[she points]* — in there?

ANTHONY: I don't mean to be.

ENID: Oh! Father, don't give them a chance. You're not well; need you go to the meeting at all?

ANTHONY: *[With a grim smile.]* Cut and run?

ENID: But they'll out-vote you!

ANTHONY: *[Putting his hand on the doors.]* We shall see!

ENID: I beg you, Dad! Won't you?
[ANTHONY looks at her softly.]

[ANTHONY shakes his head. He opens the doors. A buzz of voices comes in.]

SCANTLEBURY: Can one get dinner on that 6.30 train up?

TENCH: No, Sir, I believe not, sir.

WILDER: Well, I shall speak out; I've had enough of this.

EDGAR: *[Sharply.]* What?
[It ceases instantly. ANTHONY passes through, closing the doors behind him. ENID springs to them with a gesture of dismay. She puts her hand on the knob, and begins turning it; then goes to the fireplace, and taps her foot on the fender. Suddenly she rings the bell. FROST comes in by the door that leads into the hall.]

FROST: Yes, M'm?

ENID: When the men come, Frost, please show them in here; the hall 's cold.

FROST: I could put them in the pantry, M'm.

ENID: No. I don't want to—to offend them; they're so touchy.

FROST: Yes, M'm. *[Pause.]* Excuse me, Mr. Anthony's 'ad nothing to eat all day.

ENID: I know Frost.

FROST: Nothin' but two whiskies and sodas, M'm.

ENID: Oh! you oughtn't to have let him have those.

FROST: *[Gravely.]* Mr. Anthony is a little difficult, M'm. It's not as if he were a younger man, an' knew what was good for 'im; he will have his own way.

ENID: I suppose we all want that.

FROST: Yes, M'm. *[Quietly.]* Excuse me speakin' about the strike. I'm sure if the other gentlemen were to give up to Mr. Anthony, and quietly let the men 'ave what they want, afterwards, that'd be the best way. I find that very useful with him at times, M'm. *[ENID shakes her head.]* If he's crossed, it makes him violent, *[with an air of discovery]* and I've noticed in my own case, when I'm violent I'm always sorry for it afterwards.

ENID: *[With a smile.]* Are you ever violent, Frost?

FROST: Yes, M'm; oh! sometimes very violent.

ENID: I've never seen you.

FROST: *[Impersonally.]* No, M'm; that is so.
        [ENID fidgets towards the back of the door.]
[With feeling.] Bein' with Mr. Anthony, as you know, M'm, ever since I was fifteen, it worries me to see him crossed like this at his age. I've taken the liberty to speak to Mr. Wanklin *[dropping his voice]*—seems to be the most sensible of the gentlemen—but 'e said to me: "That's all very well, Frost, but this strike's a very serious thing," 'e said. "Serious for all parties, no doubt," I said, "but yumour 'im, sir," I said, "yumour 'im. It's like this, if a man comes to a stone wall, 'e doesn't drive 'is 'ead against it, 'e gets over it." "Yes," 'e said, "you'd better tell your master that." *[FROST looks at his nails.]* That's where it is, M'm. I said to Mr. Anthony this morning: "Is it worth it, sir?" "Damn it," he said to me, "Frost! Mind your own business, or take a month's notice!" Beg pardon, M'm, for using such a word.

ENID: *[Moving to the double-doors, and listening.]* Do you know that man Roberts, Frost?

FROST: Yes, M'm; that's to say, not to speak to. But to look at 'im you can tell what he's like.

ENID: *[Stopping.]* Yes?

FROST: He's not one of these 'ere ordinary 'armless Socialists. 'E's violent; got a fire inside 'im. What I call "personal." A man may 'ave what opinions 'e likes, so long as 'e 's not personal; when 'e 's that 'e 's not safe.

ENID: I think that's what my father feels about Roberts.

FROST: No doubt, M'm, Mr. Anthony has a feeling against him.
            *[ENID glances at him sharply, but finding him in perfect earnest,
            stands biting her lips, and looking at the double-doors.]*
It's, a regular right down struggle between the two. I've no patience with this Roberts, from what I 'ear he's just an ordinary workin' man like the rest of 'em. If he did invent a thing he's no worse off than 'undreds of others. My brother invented a new kind o' dumb-waiter—nobody gave him anything for it, an' there it is, bein' used all over the place.
            [ENID moves closer to the double-doors.]
There's a kind o' man that never forgives the world, because 'e wasn't born a gentleman. What I say is—no man that's a gentleman looks down on another because 'e 'appens to be a class or two above 'im, no more than if 'e 'appens to be a class or two below.

ENID: *[With slight impatience.]* Yes, I know, Frost, of course. Will you please go in and ask if they'll have some tea; say I sent you.

FROST: Yes, M'm.
            *[He opens the doors gently and goes in. There is a momentary
            sound of earnest, gather angry talk.]*

WILDER: I don't agree with you.

WANKLIN: We've had this over a dozen times.

EDGAR: *[Impatiently.]* Well, what's the proposition?

SCANTLEBURY: Yes, what does your father say? Tea? Not for me, not for me!

WANKLIN: What I understand the Chairman to say is this—
            [FROST re-enters closing the door behind him.]

ENID: *[Moving from the door.]* Won't they have any tea, Frost?
            *[She goes to the little table, and remains motionless, looking at
            the baby's frock.]*

[A parlourmaid enters from the hall.]

PARLOURMAID: A Miss Thomas, M'm

ENID: *[Raising her head.]* Thomas? What Miss Thomas—d' you mean a—?

PARLOURMAID: Yes, M'm.

ENID: *[Blankly.]* Oh! Where is she?

PARLOURMAID: In the porch.

ENID: I don't want— *[She hesitates.]*

FROST: Shall I dispose of her, M'm?

ENID: I'll come out. No, show her in here, Ellen.
        *[The PARLOUR MAID and FROST go out. ENID pursing her
        lips, sits at the little table, taking up the baby's frock. The
        PARLOURMAID ushers in MADGE THOMAS and goes out;
        MADGE stands by the door.]*

ENID: Come in. What is it. What have you come for, please?

MADGE: Brought a message from Mrs. Roberts.

ENID: A message? Yes.

MADGE: She asks you to look after her mother.

ENID: I don't understand.

MADGE: *[Sullenly.]* That's the message.

ENID: But—what—why?

MADGE: Annie Roberts is dead.
        [There is a silence.]

ENID: *[Horrified.]* But it's only a little more than an hour since I saw her.

MADGE: Of cold and hunger.

ENID: *[Rising.]* Oh! that's not true! the poor thing's heart—What makes you look at me like that? I tried to help her.

MADGE: *[With suppressed savagery.]* I thought you'd like to know.

ENID: *[Passionately.]* It's so unjust! Can't you see that I want to help you all?

MADGE: I never harmed any one that hadn't harmed me first.

ENID: *[Coldly.]* What harm have I done you? Why do you speak to me like that?

MADGE: *[With the bitterest intensity.]* You come out of your comfort to spy on us! A week of hunger, that's what you want!

ENID: *[Standing her ground.]* Don't talk nonsense!

MADGE: I saw her die; her hands were blue with the cold.

ENID: *[With a movement of grief.]* Oh! why wouldn't she let me help her? It's such senseless pride!

MADGE: Pride's better than nothing to keep your body warm.

ENID: *[Passionately.]* I won't talk to you! How can you tell what I feel? It's not my fault that I was born better off than you.

MADGE: We don't want your money.

ENID: You don't understand, and you don't want to; please to go away!

MADGE: *[Balefully.]* You've killed her, for all your soft words, you and your father!

ENID: *[With rage and emotion.]* That's wicked! My father is suffering himself through this wretched strike.

MADGE: *[With sombre triumph.]* Then tell him Mrs. Roberts is dead! That'll make him better.

ENID: Go away!

MADGE: When a person hurts us we get it back on them.
        *[She makes a sudden and swift movement towards ENID, fixing
        her eyes on the child's frock lying across the little table. ENID
        snatches the frock up, as though it were the child itself. They
        stand a yard apart, crossing glances.]*

MADGE: *[Pointing to the frock with a little smile.]* Ah! You felt that!
Lucky it's her mother—not her children—you've to look after, isn't it. She
won't trouble you long!

ENID: Go away!

MADGE: I've given you the message.
        *[She turns and goes out into the hall. ENID, motionless till she
        has gone, sinks down at the table, bending her head over the
        frock, which she is still clutching to her. The double-doors are
        opened, and ANTHONY comes slowly in; he passes his daughter,
        and lowers himself into an arm-chair. He is very flushed.]*

ENID: *[Hiding her emotion-anxiously.]* What is it, Dad?
        [ANTHONY makes a gesture, but does not speak.]
Who was it?
        *[ANTHONY does not answer. ENID going to the double-doors
        meets EDGAR Coming in. They speak together in low tones.]*
What is it, Ted?

EDGAR: That fellow Wilder! Taken to personalities! He was downright
insulting.

ENID: What did he say?

EDGAR: Said, Father was too old and feeble to know what he was doing!
Dad's worth six of him!

ENID: Of course he is.
        *[They look at ANTHONY. The doors open wider, WANKLIN
        appears With SCANTLEBURY.]*

SCANTLEBURY: *[Sotto voce.]* I don't like the look of this!

WANKLIN: *[Going forward.]* Come, Chairman! Wilder sends you his apologies. A man can't do more.
> *[WILDER, followed by TENCH, comes in, and goes to ANTHONY.]*

WILDER: *[Glumly.]* I withdraw my words, sir. I'm sorry.
> *[ANTHONY nods to him.]*

ENID: You haven't come to a decision, Mr. Wanklin?
> *[WANKLIN shakes his head.]*

WANKLIN: We're all here, Chairman; what do you say? Shall we get on with the business, or shall we go back to the other room?

SCANTLEBURY: Yes, yes; let's get on. We must settle something.
> *[He turns from a small chair, and settles himself suddenly in the largest chair with a sigh of comfort. WILDER and WANKLIN also sit; and TENCH, drawing up a straight-backed chair close to his Chairman, sits on the edge of it with the minute-book and a stylographic pen.]*

ENID: *[Whispering.]* I want to speak to you a minute, Ted.
> *[They go out through the double-doors.]*

WANKLIN: Really, Chairman, it's no use soothing ourselves with a sense of false security. If this strike's not brought to an end before the General Meeting, the shareholders will certainly haul us over the coals.

SCANTLEBURY: *[Stirring.]* What—what's that?

WANKLIN: I know it for a fact.

ANTHONY: Let them!

WILDER: And get turned out?

WANKLIN: *[To ANTHONY.]* I don't mind martyrdom for a policy in which I believe, but I object to being burnt for someone else's principles.

SCANTLEBURY: Very reasonable—you must see that, Chairman.

ANTHONY: We owe it to other employers to stand firm.

WANKLIN: There's a limit to that.

ANTHONY: You were all full of fight at the start.

SCANTLEBURY: *[With a sort of groan.]* We thought the men would give in, but they haven't!

ANTHONY: They will!

WILDER: *[Rising and pacing up and down.]* I can't have my reputation as a man of business destroyed for the satisfaction of starving the men out. *[Almost in tears.]* I can't have it! How can we meet the shareholders with things in the state they are?

SCANTLEBURY: Hear, hear—hear, hear!

WILDER: *[Lashing himself.]* If any one expects me to say to them I've lost you fifty thousand pounds and sooner than put my pride in my pocket I'll lose you another. *[Glancing at ANTHONY.]* It's—it's unnatural! I don't want to go against you, sir.

WANKLIN: *[Persuasively.]* Come Chairman, we're not free agents. We're part of a machine. Our only business is to see the Company earns as much profit as it safely can. If you blame me for want of principle: I say that we're Trustees. Reason tells us we shall never get back in the saving of wages what we shall lose if we continue this struggle—really, Chairman, we must bring it to an end, on the best terms we can make.

ANTHONY: No.
          [There is a pause of general dismay.]

WILDER: It's a deadlock then. *[Letting his hands drop with a sort of despair.]* Now I shall never get off to Spain!

WANKLIN: *[Retaining a trace of irony.]* You hear the consequences of your victory, Chairman?

WILDER: *[With a burst of feeling.]* My wife's ill!

SCANTLEBURY: Dear, dear! You don't say so.

WILDER: If I don't get her out of this cold, I won't answer for the consequences.

> *[Through the double-doors EDGAR comes in looking very grave.]*

EDGAR. [To his Father.] Have you heard this, sir? Mrs. Roberts is dead!

> *[Everyone stares at him, as if trying to gauge the importance of this news.]*

Enid saw her this afternoon, she had no coals, or food, or anything. It's enough!

> *[There is a silence, every one avoiding the other's eyes, except ANTHONY, who stares hard at his son.]*

SCANTLEBURY: You don't suggest that we could have helped the poor thing?

WILDER: *[Flustered.]* The woman was in bad health. Nobody can say there's any responsibility on us. At least—not on me.

EDGAR: *[Hotly.]* I say that we are responsible.

ANTHONY: War is war!

EDGAR: Not on women!

WANKLIN: It not infrequently happens that women are the greatest sufferers.

EDGAR: If we knew that, all the more responsibility rests on us.

ANTHONY: This is no matter for amateurs.

EDGAR: Call me what you like, sir. It's sickened me. We had no right to carry things to such a length.

WILDER: I don't like this business a bit—that Radical rag will twist it to their own ends; see if they don't! They'll get up some cock and bull story about the poor woman's dying from starvation. I wash my hands of it.

EDGAR: You can't. None of us can.

SCANTLEBURY: *[Striking his fist on the arm of his chair.]* But I protest against this!

EDGAR: Protest as you like, Mr. Scantlebury, it won't alter facts.

ANTHONY: That's enough.

EDGAR: *[Facing him angrily.]* No, sir. I tell you exactly what I think. If we pretend the men are not suffering, it's humbug; and if they're suffering, we know enough of human nature to know the women are suffering more, and as to the children—well—it's damnable!
    [SCANTLEBURY rises from his chair.]
I don't say that we meant to be cruel, I don't say anything of the sort; but I do say it's criminal to shut our eyes to the facts. We employ these men, and we can't get out of it. I don't care so much about the men, but I'd sooner resign my position on the Board than go on starving women in this way.
    [All except ANTHONY are now upon their feet, ANTHONY sits grasping the arms of his chair and staring at his son.]

SCANTLEBURY: I don't—I don't like the way you're putting it, young sir.

WANKLIN: You're rather overshooting the mark.

WILDER: I should think so indeed!

EDGAR: *[Losing control.]* It's no use blinking things! If you want to have the death of women on your hands—I don't!

SCANTLEBURY: Now, now, young man!

WILDER: On our hands? Not on mine, I won't have it!

EDGAR: We are five members of this Board; if we were four against it, why did we let it drift till it came to this? You know perfectly well why—because we hoped we should starve the men out. Well, all we've done is to starve one woman out!

SCANTLEBURY: *[Almost hysterically.]* I protest, I protest! I'm a humane man—we're all humane men!

EDGAR: *[Scornfully.]* There's nothing wrong with our humanity. It's our imaginations, Mr. Scantlebury.

WILDER: Nonsense! My imagination's as good as yours.

EDGAR: If so, it isn't good enough.

WILDER: I foresaw this!

EDGAR: Then why didn't you put your foot down!

WILDER: Much good that would have done.
      [He looks at ANTHONY.]

EDGAR: If you, and I, and each one of us here who say that our imaginations are so good—

SCANTLEBURY: *[Flurried.]* I never said so.

EDGAR: *[Paying no attention.]* —had put our feet down, the thing would have been ended long ago, and this poor woman's life wouldn't have been crushed out of her like this. For all we can tell there may be a dozen other starving women.

SCANTLEBURY: For God's sake, sir, don't use that word at a—at a Board meeting; it's—it's monstrous.

EDGAR: I will use it, Mr. Scantlebury.

SCANTLEBURY: Then I shall not listen to you. I shall not listen! It's painful to me.
      [He covers his ears.]

WANKLIN: None of us are opposed to a settlement, except your Father.

EDGAR: I'm certain that if the shareholders knew—

WANKLIN: I don't think you'll find their imaginations are any better than ours. Because a woman happens to have a weak heart—

EDGAR: A struggle like this finds out the weak spots in everybody. Any child knows that. If it hadn't been for this cut-throat policy, she needn't have died like this; and there wouldn't be all this misery that anyone who isn't a fool can see is going on.

*[Throughout the foregoing ANTHONY has eyed his son; he now
moves as though to rise, but stops as EDGAR speaks again.]*
I don't defend the men, or myself, or anybody.

WANKLIN: You may have to! A coroner's jury of disinterested
sympathisers may say some very nasty things. We mustn't lose sight of our
position.

SCANTLEBURY: *[Without uncovering his ears.]* Coroner's jury! No, no,
it's not a case for that!

EDGAR: I've had enough of cowardice.

WANKLIN: Cowardice is an unpleasant word, Mr. Edgar Anthony. It will
look very like cowardice if we suddenly concede the men's demands when a
thing like this happens; we must be careful!

WILDER: Of course we must. We've no knowledge of this matter, except a
rumour. The proper course is to put the whole thing into the hands of
Harness to settle for us; that's natural, that's what we should have come to
anyway.

SCANTLEBURY: *[With dignity.]* Exactly! *[Turning to EDGAR.]* And as
to you, young sir, I can't sufficiently express my—my distaste for the way
you've treated the whole matter. You ought to withdraw! Talking of
starvation, talking of cowardice! Considering what our views are! Except
your own is—is one of goodwill—it's most irregular, it's most improper, and
all I can say is it's—it's given me pain—
        [He places his hand over his heart.]

EDGAR: *[Stubbornly.]* I withdraw nothing.

        *[He is about to say more when SCANTLEBURY once more covers
        up his ears. TENCH suddenly makes a demonstration with the
        minute-book. A sense of having been engaged in the unusual
        comes over all of them, and one by one they resume their seats.
        EDGAR alone remains on his feet.]*

WILDER: *[With an air of trying to wipe something out.]* I pay no attention
to what young Mr. Anthony has said. Coroner's jury! The idea's
preposterous. I—I move this amendment to the Chairman's Motion: That
the dispute be placed at once in the hands of Mr. Simon Harness for

settlement, on the lines indicated by him this morning. Any one second that?

> *[TENCH writes in his book.]*

WANKLIN: I do.

WILDER: Very well, then; I ask the Chairman to put it to the Board.

ANTHONY: *[With a great sigh-slowly.]* We have been made the subject of an attack. *[Looking round at WILDER and SCANTLEBURY with ironical contempt.]* I take it on my shoulders. I am seventy-six years old. I have been Chairman of this Company since its inception two-and-thirty years ago. I have seen it pass through good and evil report. My connection with it began in the year that this young man was born.

> *[EDGAR bows his head. ANTHONY, gripping his chair, goes on.]*

I have had do to with "men" for fifty years; I've always stood up to them; I have never been beaten yet. I have fought the men of this Company four times, and four times I have beaten them. It has been said that I am not the man I was. *[He looks at Wilder.]* However that may be, I am man enough to stand to my guns.

> *[His voice grows stronger. The double-doors are opened. ENID slips in, followed by UNDERWOOD, who restrains her.]*

The men have been treated justly, they have had fair wages, we have always been ready to listen to complaints. It has been said that times have changed; if they have, I have not changed with them. Neither will I. It has been said that masters and men are equal! Cant! There can only be one master in a house! Where two men meet the better man will rule. It has been said that Capital and Labour have the same interests. Cant! Their interests are as wide asunder as the poles. It has been said that the Board is only part of a machine. Cant! We are the machine; its brains and sinews; it is for us to lead and to determine what is to be done, and to do it without fear or favour. Fear of the men! Fear of the shareholders! Fear of our own shadows! Before I am like that, I hope to die.

> *[He pauses, and meeting his son's eyes, goes on.]*

There is only one way of treating "men"—with the iron hand. This half and half business, the half and half manners of this generation, has brought all this upon us. Sentiment and softness, and what this young man, no doubt, would call his social policy. You can't eat cake and have it! This middle-class sentiment, or socialism, or whatever it may be, is rotten. Masters are masters, men are men! Yield one demand, and they will make it six. They are *[he smiles grimly]* like Oliver Twist, asking for more. If I were in their place I should be the same. But I am not in their place. Mark my words: one fine morning, when you have given way here, and given way there— you will find you have parted with the ground beneath your feet, and are deep in the bog of bankruptcy; and with you, floundering in that bog, will be the very men you have given way to. I have been accused of being a domineering tyrant, thinking only of my pride—I am thinking of the future of this country, threatened with the black waters of confusion, threatened with mob government, threatened with what I cannot see. If by any conduct of mine I help to bring this on us, I shall be ashamed to look my fellows in the face.

> [ANTHONY stares before him, at what he cannot see, and there is perfect stillness. FROST comes in from the hall, and all but ANTHONY look round at him uneasily.]

FROST: [To his master.] The men are here, sir. [ANTHONY makes a gesture of dismissal.] Shall I bring them in, sir?

ANTHONY: Wait!

> [FROST goes out, ANTHONY turns to face his son.]

I come to the attack that has been made upon me.

> [EDGAR, with a gesture of deprecation, remains motionless with his head a little bowed.]

A woman has died. I am told that her blood is on my hands; I am told that on my hands is the starvation and the suffering of other women and of children.

EDGAR: I said "on our hands," sir.

ANTHONY: It is the same. [His voice grows stronger and stronger, his feeling is more and more made manifest.] I am not aware that if my adversary suffer in a fair fight not sought by me, it is my fault. If I fall under his feet—as fall I may—I shall not complain. That will be my look-out—and this is—his. I cannot separate, as I would, these men from their women and children. A fair fight is a fair fight! Let them learn to think before they pick a quarrel!

EDGAR: [In a low voice.] But is it a fair fight, Father? Look at them, and look at us! They've only this one weapon!

ANTHONY: [Grimly.] And you're weak-kneed enough to teach them how to use it! It seems the fashion nowadays for men to take their enemy's side.

I have not learnt that art. Is it my fault that they quarreled with their Union too?

EDGAR: There is such a thing as Mercy.

ANTHONY: And justice comes before it.

EDGAR: What seems just to one man, sir, is injustice to another.

ANTHONY: *[With suppressed passion.]* You accuse me of injustice—of what amounts to inhumanity—of cruelty?
> *[EDGAR makes a gesture of horror—a general frightened movement.]*

WANKLIN: Come, come, Chairman.

ANTHONY: *[In a grim voice.]* These are the words of my own son. They are the words of a generation that I don't understand; the words of a soft breed.
> *[A general murmur. With a violent effort ANTHONY recovers his control.]*

EDGAR: *[Quietly.]* I said it of myself, too, Father.
> *[A long look is exchanged between them, and ANTHONY puts out his hand with a gesture as if to sweep the personalities away; then places it against his brow, swaying as though from giddiness. There is a movement towards him. He moves them back.]*

ANTHONY: Before I put this amendment to the Board, I have one more word to say. *[He looks from face to face.]* If it is carried, it means that we shall fail in what we set ourselves to do. It means that we shall fail in the duty that we owe to all Capital. It means that we shall fail in the duty that we owe ourselves. It means that we shall be open to constant attack to which we as constantly shall have to yield. Be under no misapprehension—run this time, and you will never make a stand again! You will have to fly like curs before the whips of your own men. If that is the lot you wish for, you will vote for this amendment.
> *[He looks again, from face to face, finally resting his gaze on EDGAR; all sit with their eyes on the ground. ANTHONY makes a gesture, and TENCH hands him the book. He reads.]*

"Moved by Mr. Wilder, and seconded by Mr. Wanklin: 'That the men's demands be placed at once in the hands of Mr. Simon Harness for settlement

on the lines indicated by him this morning.'" *[With sudden vigour.]* Those
in favour: Signify the same in the usual way!
> *[For a minute no one moves; then hastily, just as ANTHONY is
> about to speak, WILDER's hand and WANKLIN'S are held up,
> then SCANTLEBURY'S, and last EDGAR'S who does not lift his
> head.]*

> *[ANTHONY lifts his own hand.]*

ANTHONY: *[In a clear voice.]* The amendment is carried. I resign my
position on this Board.
> *[ENID gasps, and there is dead silence. ANTHONY sits
> motionless, his head slowly drooping; suddenly he heaves as
> though the whole of his life had risen up within him.]*

Fifty years! You have disgraced me, gentlemen. Bring in the men!
> *[He sits motionless, staring before him. The Board draws
> hurriedly together, and forms a group. TENCH in a frightened
> manner speaks into the hall. UNDERWOOD almost forces ENID
> from the room.]*

WILDER: *[Hurriedly.]* What's to be said to them? Why isn't Harness here?
Ought we to see the men before he comes? I don't—

TENCH: Will you come in, please?
> *[Enter THOMAS, GREEN, BULGIN, and ROUS, who file up in a
> row past the little table. TENCH sits down and writes. All eyes
> are foxed on ANTHONY, who makes no sign.]*

WANKLIN: *[Stepping up to the little table, with nervous cordiality.]* Well,
Thomas, how's it to be? What's the result of your meeting?

ROUS: Sim Harness has our answer. He'll tell you what it is. We're waiting
for him. He'll speak for us.

WANKLIN: Is that so, Thomas?

THOMAS: *[Sullenly.]* Yes. Roberts will not pe coming, his wife is dead.

SCANTLEBURY: Yes, yes! Poor woman! Yes! Yes!

FROST: *[Entering from the hall.]* Mr. Harness, Sir!

[As HARNESS enters he retires.]

[HARNESS has a piece of paper in his hand, he bows to the Directors, nods towards the men, and takes his stand behind the little table in the very centre of the room.]

HARNESS: Good evening, gentlemen.
 [TENCH, with the paper he has been writing, joins him, they speak together in low tones.]

WILDER: We've been waiting for you, Harness. Hope we shall come to some—

FROST: *[Entering from the hall.]* Roberts!
 [He goes.]

 [ROBERTS comes hastily in, and stands staring at ANTHONY. His face is drawn and old.]

ROBERTS: Mr. Anthony, I am afraid I am a little late, I would have been here in time but for something that—has happened. *[To the men.]* Has anything been said?

THOMAS: No! But, man, what made ye come?

ROBERTS: Ye told us this morning, gentlemen, to go away and reconsider our position. We have reconsidered it; we are here to bring you the men's answer. *[To ANTHONY.]* Go ye back to London. We have nothing for you. By no jot or tittle do we abate our demands, nor will we until the whole of those demands are yielded.
 [ANTHONY looks at him but does not speak. There is a movement amongst the men as though they were bewildered.]

HARNESS: Roberts!

ROBERTS: *[Glancing fiercely at him, and back to ANTHONY.]* Is that clear enough for ye? Is it short enough and to the point? Ye made a mistake to think that we would come to heel. Ye may break the body, but ye cannot break the spirit. Get back to London, the men have nothing for ye?
 [Pausing uneasily he takes a step towards the unmoving ANTHONY.]

EDGAR: We're all sorry for you, Roberts, but—

ROBERTS. Keep your sorrow, young man. Let your father speak!

HARNESS: *[With the sheet of paper in his hand, speaking from behind the little table.]* Roberts!

ROBERT: *[TO ANTHONY, with passionate intensity.]* Why don't ye answer?

HARNESS: Roberts!

ROBERTS: *[Turning sharply.]* What is it?

HARNESS: *[Gravely.]* You're talking without the book; things have travelled past you.
> *[He makes a sign to TENCH, who beckons the Directors. They quickly sign his copy of the terms.]*
Look at this, man! *[Holding up his sheet of paper.]* "Demands conceded, with the exception of those relating to the engineers and furnace-men. Double wages for Saturday's overtime. Night-shifts as they are." These terms have been agreed. The men go back to work again to-morrow. The strike is at an end.

ROBERTS: *[Reading the paper, and turning on the men. They shrink back from him, all but ROUS, who stands his ground. With deadly stillness.]* Ye have gone back on me? I stood by ye to the death; ye waited for that to throw me over!
> *[The men answer, all speaking together.]*

ROUS: It's a lie!

THOMAS: Ye were past endurance, man.

GREEN: If ye'd listen to me!

BULGIN: *[Under his breath.]* Hold your jaw!

ROBERTS: Ye waited for that!

HARNESS: *[Taking the Director's copy of the terms, and handing his own to TENCH.]* That's enough, men. You had better go.

[The men shuffle slowly, awkwardly away.]

WILDER: *[In a low, nervous voice.]* There's nothing to stay for now, I suppose. *[He follows to the door.]* I shall have a try for that train! Coming, Scantlebury?

SCANTLEBURY: *[Following with WANKLIN.]* Yes, yes; wait for me.
        [He stops as ROBERTS speaks.]

ROBERTS: *[To ANTHONY.]* But ye have not signed them terms! They can't make terms without their Chairman! Ye would never sign them terms! *[ANTHONY looks at him without speaking.]* Don't tell me ye have! for the love o' God! *[With passionate appeal.]* I reckoned on ye!

HARNESS: *[Holding out the Director's copy of the terms.]* The Board has signed!
        [ROBERTS looks dully at the signatures—dashes the paper from him, and covers up his eyes.]

SCANTLEBURY: *[Behind his hand to TENCH.]* Look after the Chairman! He's not well; he's not well—he had no lunch. If there's any fund started for the women and children, put me down for—for twenty pounds.
        [He goes out into the hall, in cumbrous haste; and WANKLIN, who has been staring at ROBERTS and ANTHONY with twitchings of his face, follows. EDGAR remains seated on the sofa, looking at the ground; TENCH, returning to the bureau, writes in his minute-book. HARNESS stands by the little table, gravely watching ROBERTS.]

ROBERTS: Then you're no longer Chairman of this Company*! [Breaking into half-mad laughter.]* Ah! ha-ah, ha, ha! They've thrown ye over— thrown over their Chairman: Ah-ha-ha! *[With a sudden dreadful calm.]* So—they've done us both down, Mr. Anthony?
        [ENID, hurrying through the double-doors, comes quickly to her father.]

ANTHONY: Both broken men, my friend Roberts!

HARNESS: *[Coming down and laying his hands on ROBERTS'S sleeve.]* For shame, Roberts! Go home quietly, man; go home!

ROBERTS: *[Tearing his arm away.]* Home? *[Shrinking together—in a whisper.]* Home!

ENID: *[Quietly to her father.]* Come away, dear! Come to your room
    *[ANTHONY rises with an effort. He turns to ROBERTS who
    looks at him. They stand several seconds, gazing at each other
    fixedly; ANTHONY lifts his hand, as though to salute, but lets it
    fall. The expression of ROBERTS' face changes from hostility to
    wonder. They bend their heads in token of respect. ANTHONY
    turns, and slowly walks towards the curtained door. Suddenly he
    sways as though about to fall, recovers himself, and is assisted
    out by EDGAR and ENID; UNDERWOOD follows, but stops at
    the door. ROBERTS remains motionless for several seconds,
    staring intently after ANTHONY, then goes out into the hall.]*

TENCH: *[Approaching HARNESS.]* It's a great weight off my mind, Mr.
Harness! But what a painful scene, sir! *[He wipes his brow.]*
    *[HARNESS, pale and resolute, regards with a grim half-smile the
    quavering.]*

TENCH: It's all been so violent! What did he mean by: "Done us both
down?" If he has lost his wife, poor fellow, he oughtn't to have spoken to
the Chairman like that!

HARNESS: A woman dead; and the two best men both broken!

TENCH: *[Staring at him—suddenly excited.]* D'you know, sir—these
terms, they're the very same we drew up together, you and I, and put to both
sides before the fight began? All this—all this—and—and what for?

HARNESS: *[In a slow grim voice.]* That's where the fun comes in!
    *[UNDERWOOD without turning from the door makes a gesture
    of assent.]*

                        The curtain falls.

DEFEAT

A TINY DRAMA

CHARACTERS

———◈———

THE OFFICER
THE GIRL

DEFEAT

During the Great War. Evening.

[An empty room. The curtains drawn and gas turned low. The furniture and walls give a colour-impression as of greens and beetroot. There is a prevalence of plush. A fireplace on the Left, a sofa, a small table; the curtained window is at the back. On the table, in a common pot, stands a little plant of maidenhair fern, fresh and green.]

[Enter from the door on the Right, a GIRL and a YOUNG OFFICER in khaki. The GIRL wears a discreet dark dress, hat, and veil, and stained yellow gloves. The YOUNG OFFICER is tall, with a fresh open face, and kindly eager blue eyes; he is a little lame. The GIRL, who is evidently at home, moves towards the gas jet to turn it up, then changes her mind, and going to the curtains, draws them apart and throws up the window. Bright moonlight comes flooding in. Outside are seen the trees of a little Square. She stands gazing out, suddenly turns inward with a shiver.]

YOUNG OFFICER: I say; what's the matter? You were crying when I spoke to you.

GIRL: *[With a movement of recovery]* Oh! nothing. The beautiful evening—that's all.

YOUNG OFFICER: *[Looking at her]* Cheer up!

GIRL: *[Taking of hat and veil; her hair is yellowish and crinkly]* Cheer up! You are not lonelee, like me.

YOUNG OFFICER: *[Limping to the window—doubtfully]* I say, how did you—how did you get into this? Isn't it an awfully hopeless sort of life?

GIRL: Yees, it ees. You haf been wounded?

YOUNG OFFICER: Just out of hospital to-day.

89

GIRL: The horrible war—all the misery is because of the war. When will it end?

YOUNG OFFICER: *[Leaning against the window-sill, looking at her attentively]* I say, what nationality are you?

GIRL: *[With a quick look and away]* Rooshian.

YOUNG OFFICER: Really! I never met a Russian girl. *[The GIRL gives him another quick look]* I say, is it as bad as they make out?

GIRL: *[Slipping her hand through his arm]* Not when I haf anyone as ni-ice as you; I never haf had, though. *[She smiles, and her smile, like her speech, is slow and confining]* You stopped because I was sad, others stop because I am gay. I am not fond of men at all. When you know—you are not fond of them.

YOUNG OFFICER: Well, you hardly know them at their best, do you? You should see them in the trenches. By George! They're simply splendid—officers and men, every blessed soul. There's never been anything like it—just one long bit of jolly fine self-sacrifice; it's perfectly amazing.

GIRL: *[Turning her blue-grey eyes on him]* I expect you are not the last at that. You see in them what you haf in yourself, I think.

YOUNG OFFICER: Oh, not a bit; you're quite out! I assure you when we made the attack where I got wounded there wasn't a single man in my regiment who wasn't an absolute hero. The way they went in—never thinking of themselves—it was simply ripping.

GIRL: *[In a queer voice]* It is the same too, perhaps, with—the enemy.

YOUNG OFFICER: Oh, yes! I know that.

GIRL: Ah! You are not a mean man. How I hate mean men!

YOUNG OFF: Oh! they're not mean really—they simply don't understand.

GIRL: Oh! You are a babe—a good babee aren't you?
   [The YOUNG OFFICER doesn't like this, and frowns. The GIRL looks a little scared.]

GIRL: *[Clingingly]* But I li-ke you for it. It is so good to find a
ni-ice man.

YOUNG OFFICER: *[Abruptly]* About being lonely? Haven't you any
Russian friends?

GIRL: *[Blankly]* Rooshian? No. *[Quickly]* The town is so beeg. Were
you at the concert before you spoke to me?

YOUNG OFFICER: Yes.

GIRL: I too. I lofe music.

YOUNG OFFICER: I suppose all Russians do.

GIRL: *[With another quick look at him]* I go there always when I haf the
money.

YOUNG OFFICER: What! Are you as badly on the rocks as that?

GIRL: Well, I haf just one shilling now!
        *[She laughs bitterly. The laugh upsets him; he sits on the
        window-sill, and leans forward towards her.]*

YOUNG OFFICER: I say, what's your name?

GIRL: May. Well, I call myself that. It is no good asking yours.

YOUNG OFFICER: *[With a laugh]* You're a distrustful little soul; aren't
you?

GIRL: I haf reason to be, don't you think?

YOUNG OFFICER: Yes. I suppose you're bound to think us all brutes.

GIRL: *[Sitting on a chair close to the window where the moonlight falls on
one powdered cheek]* Well, I haf a lot of reasons to be afraid all my time. I
am dreadfully nervous now; I am not trusding anybody. I suppose you haf
been killing lots of Germans?

YOUNG OFFICER: We never know, unless it happens to be hand to hand; I
haven't come in for that yet.

GIRL: But you would be very glad if you had killed some.

YOUNG OFFICER: Oh, glad? I don't think so. We're all in the same boat, so far as that's concerned. We're not glad to kill each other—not most of us. We do our job—that's all.

GIRL: Oh! It is frightful. I expect I haf my brothers killed.

YOUNG OFFICER: Don't you get any news ever?

GIRL: News? No indeed, no news of anybody in my country. I might not haf a country; all that I ever knew is gone; fader, moder, sisters, broders, all; never any more I shall see them, I suppose, now. The war it breaks and breaks, it breaks hearts. *[She gives a little snarl]* Do you know what I was thinking when you came up to me? I was thinking of my native town, and the river in the moonlight. If I could see it again I would be glad. Were you ever homeseeck?

YOUNG OFFICER: Yes, I have been—in the trenches. But one's ashamed with all the others.

GIRL: Ah! Yees! Yees! You are all comrades there. What is it like for me here, do you think, where everybody hates and despises me, and would catch me and put me in prison, perhaps. *[Her breast heaves.]*

YOUNG OFFICER: *[Leaning forward and patting her knee]* Sorry—sorry.

GIRL: *[In a smothered voice]* You are the first who has been kind to me for so long! I will tell you the truth—I am not Rooshian at all—I am German.

YOUNG OFFICER: *[Staring]* My dear girl, who cares. We aren't fighting against women.

GIRL: *[Peering at him]* Another man said that to me. But he was thinkin' of his fun. You are a veree ni-ice boy; I am so glad I met you. You see the good in people, don't you? That is the first thing in the world—because— there is really not much good in people, you know.

YOUNG OFFICER: *[Smiling]* You are a dreadful little cynic! But of course you are!

GIRL: Cyneec? How long do you think I would live if I was not a cyneec? I should drown myself to-morrow. Perhaps there are good people, but, you see, I don't know them.

YOUNG OFFICER: I know lots.

GIRL: *[Leaning towards him]* Well now—see, ni-ice boy—you haf never been in a hole, haf you?

YOUNG OFFICER: I suppose not a real hole.

GIRL: No, I should think not, with your face. Well, suppose I am still a good girl, as I was once, you know; and you took me to your mother and your sisters and you said: "Here is a little German girl that has no work, and no money, and no friends." They will say: "Oh! how sad! A German girl!" And they will go and wash their hands.
    [The OFFICER, is silent, staring at her.]

GIRL: You see.

YOUNG OFFICER: *[Muttering]* I'm sure there are people.

GIRL: No. They would not take a German, even if she was good. Besides, I don't want to be good any more—I am not a humbug; I have learned to be bad. Aren't you going to kees me, ni-ice boy?
    [She puts her face close to his. Her eyes trouble him; he draws back.]

YOUNG OFFICER: Don't. I'd rather not, if you don't mind. *[She looks at him fixedly, with a curious inquiring stare]* It's stupid. I don't know—but you see, out there, and in hospital, life's different. It's—it's—it isn't mean, you know. Don't come too close.

GIRL: Oh! You are fun— *[She stops]* Eesn't it light. No Zeps to-night. When they burn—what a 'orrble death! And all the people cheer. It is natural. Do you hate us veree much?

YOUNG OFFICER: *[Turning sharply]* Hate? I don't know.

GIRL: I don't hate even the English—I despise them. I despise my people too; even more, because they began this war. Oh! I know that. I despise all the peoples. Why haf they made the world so miserable—why haf they

killed all our lives—hundreds and thousands and millions of lives—all for
noting? They haf made a bad world—everybody hating, and looking for the
worst everywhere. They haf made me bad, I know. I believe no more in
anything. What is there to believe in? Is there a God? No! Once I was
teaching little English children their prayers—isn't that funnee? I was
reading to them about Christ and love. I believed all those things. Now I
believe noting at all—no one who is not a fool or a liar can believe. I would
like to work in a 'ospital; I would like to go and 'elp poor boys like you.
Because I am a German they would throw me out a 'undred times, even if I
was good. It is the same in Germany, in France, in Russia, everywhere. But
do you think I will believe in Love and Christ and God and all that—Not I!
I think we are animals—that's all! Oh, yes! you fancy it is because my life
has spoiled me. It is not that at all—that is not the worst thing in life. The
men I take are not ni-ice, like you, but it's their nature; and—they help me to
live, which is something for me, anyway. No, it is the men who think
themselves great and good and make the war with their talk and their hate,
killing us all—killing all the boys like you, and keeping poor People in
prison, and telling us to go on hating; and all these dreadful cold-blood
creatures who write in the papers—the same in my country—just the same;
it is because of all of them that I think we are only animals.
            [The YOUNG OFFICER gets up, acutely miserable.]

            [She follows him with her eyes.]

GIRL: Don't mind me talkin', ni-ice boy. I don't know anyone to talk to. If
you don't like it, I can be quiet as a mouse.

YOUNG OFFICER: Oh, go on! Talk away; I'm not obliged to believe you,
and I don't.
            *[She, too, is on her feet now, leaning against the wall; her dark
            dress and white face just touched by the slanting moonlight. Her
            voice comes again, slow and soft and bitter.]*

GIRL: Well, look here, ni-ice boy, what sort of world is it, where millions
are being tortured, for no fault of theirs, at all? A beautiful world, isn't it?
'Umbog! Silly rot, as you boys call it. You say it is all "Comrades" and
braveness out there at the front, and people don't think of themselves. Well,
I don't think of myself veree much. What does it matter? I am lost now,
anyway. But I think of my people at 'ome; how they suffer and grieve. I
think of all the poor people there, and here, how lose those they love, and all
the poor prisoners. Am I not to think of them? And if I do, how am I to
believe it a beautiful world, ni-ice boy?

[He stands very still, staring at her.]

GIRL: Look here! We haf one life each, and soon it is over. Well, I think that is lucky.

YOUNG OFFICER: No! There's more than that.

GIRL: *[Softly]* Ah! You think the war is fought for the future; you are giving your lives for a better world, aren't you?

YOUNG OFFICER: We must fight till we win.

GIRL: Till you win. My people think that too. All the peoples think that if they win the world will be better. But it will not, you know; it will be much worse, anyway.
>   *[He turns away from her, and catches up his cap. Her voice follows him.]*

GIRL: I don't care which win. I don't care if my country is beaten. I despise them all—animals—animals. Ah! Don't go, ni-ice boy; I will be quiet now.
>   *[He has taken some notes from his tunic pocket; he puts then on the table and goes up to her.]*

YOUNG OFFICER: Good-night.

GIRL: *[Plaintively]* Are you really going? Don't you like me enough?

YOUNG OFFICER: Yes, I like you.

GIRL: It is because I am German, then?

YOUNG OFFICER: No.

GIRL: Then why won't you stay?

YOUNG OFFICER: *[With a shrug]* If you must know—because you upset me.

GIRL: Won't you kees me once?
>   *[He bends, puts his lips to her forehead. But as he takes them away she throws her head back, presses her mouth to his, and clings to him.]*

YOUNG OFFICER: *[Sitting down suddenly]* Don't! I don't want to feel a brute.

GIRL: *[Laughing]* You are a funny boy; but you are veree good. Talk to me a little, then. No one talks to me. Tell me, haf you seen many German prisoners?

YOUNG OFFICER: *[Sighing]* A good many.

GIRL: Any from the Rhine?

YOUNG OFFICER: Yes, I think so.

GIRL: Were they veree sad?

YOUNG OFFICER: Some were; some were quite glad to be taken.

GIRL: Did you ever see the Rhine? It will be wonderful to-night. The moonlight will be the same there, and in Rooshia too, and France, everywhere; and the trees will look the same as here, and people will meet under them and make love just as here. Oh! isn't it stupid, the war? As if it were not good to be alive!

YOUNG OFFICER: You can't tell how good it is to be alive till you're facing death. You don't live till then. And when a whole lot of you feel like that—and are ready to give their lives for each other, it's worth all the rest of life put together.
> *[He stops, ashamed of such, sentiment before this girl, who believes in nothing.]*

GIRL: *[Softly]* How were you wounded, ni-ice boy?

YOUNG OFFICER: Attacking across open ground: four machine bullets got me at one go off.

GIRL: Weren't you veree frightened when they ordered you to attack?
> *[He shakes his head and laughs.]*

YOUNG OFFICER: It was great. We did laugh that morning. They got me much too soon, though—a swindle.

GIRL: *[Staring at him]* You laughed?

YOUNG OFFICER: Yes. And what do you think was the first thing I was conscious of next morning? My old Colonel bending over me and giving me a squeeze of lemon. If you knew my Colonel you'd still believe in things. There is something, you know, behind all this evil. After all, you can only die once, and, if it's for your country—all the better!

> *[Her face, in the moonlight, with, intent eyes touched up with black, has a most strange, other-world look.]*

GIRL: No; I believe in nothing, not even in my country. My heart is dead.

YOUNG OFFICER: Yes; you think so, but it isn't, you know, or you wouldn't have 'been crying when I met you.

GIRL: If it were not dead, do you think I could live my life—walking the streets every night, pretending to like strange men; never hearing a kind word; never talking, for fear I will be known for a German? Soon I shall take to drinking; then I shall be "Kaput" veree quick. You see, I am practical; I see things clear. To-night I am a little emotional; the moon is funny, you know. But I live for myself only, now. I don't care for anything or anybody.

YOUNG OFFICER: All the same; just now you were pitying your folk at home, and prisoners and that.

GIRL: Yees; because they suffer. Those who suffer are like me—I pity myself, that's all; I am different from your English women. I see what I am doing; I do not let my mind become a turnip just because I am no longer moral.

YOUNG OFFICER: Nor your heart either, for all you say.

GIRL: Ni-ice boy, you are veree obstinate. But all that about love is 'umbog. We love ourselves, noting more.

> *[At that intense soft bitterness in her voice, he gets up, feeling stifled, and stands at the window. A newspaper boy some way off is calling his wares. The GIRL's fingers slip between his own, and stay unmoving. He looks round into her face. In spite of make-up it has a queer, unholy, touching beauty.]*

YOUNG OFFICER: *[With an outburst]* No; we don't only love ourselves; there is more. I can't explain, but there's something great; there's kindness—and—and—

[The shouting of newspaper boys grows louder and their cries, passionately vehement, clash into each other and obscure each word. His head goes up to listen; her hand tightens within his arm—she too is listening. The cries come nearer, hoarser, more shrill and clamorous; the empty moonlight outside seems suddenly crowded with figures, footsteps, voices, and a fierce distant cheering. "Great victory—great victory! Official! British! 'Eavy defeat of the 'Uns! Many thousand prisoners! 'Eavy defeat!" It speeds by, intoxicating, filling him with a fearful joy; he leans far out, waving his cap and cheering like a madman; the night seems to flutter and vibrate and answer. He turns to rush down into the street, strikes against something soft, and recoils. The GIRL stands with hands clenched, and face convulsed, panting. All confused with the desire to do something, he stoops to kiss her hand. She snatches away her fingers, sweeps up the notes he has put down, and holds them out to him.]

GIRL: Take them—I will not haf your English money—take them.
> *[Suddenly she tears them across, twice, thrice, lets the bits flutter to the floor, and turns her back on him. He stands looking at her leaning against the plush-covered table, her head down, a dark figure in a dark room, with the moonlight sharpening her outline. Hardly a moment he stays, then makes for the door. When he is gone, she still stands there, her chin on her breast, with the sound in her ears of cheering, of hurrying feet, and voices crying: "'Eavy Defeat!" stands, in the centre of a pattern made by the fragments of the torn-up notes, staring out unto the moonlight, seeing not this hated room and the hated Square outside, but a German orchard, and herself, a little girl, plucking apples, a big dog beside her; and a hundred other pictures, such as the drowning see. Then she sinks down on the floor, lays her forehead on the dusty carpet, and presses her body to it. Mechanically, she sweeps together the scattered fragments of notes, assembling them with the dust into a little pile, as of fallen leaves, and dabbling in it with her fingers, while the tears run down her cheeks.]*

Defeat! Der Vaterland! Defeat! . . . One shillin'!
> *[Then suddenly, in the moonlight, she sits up, and begins to sing with all her might "Die Wacht am Rhein." And outside men pass, singing: "Rule, Britannia!"]*

CURTAIN

THE FIRST AND THE LAST

A DRAMA IN THREE SCENES

CHARACTERS

———◆———

KEITH DARRANT, *K.C.*
LARRY DARRANT, *his brother*
WANDA

THE FIRST AND THE LAST

SCENE I. Keith's study.

[It is six o'clock of a November evening, in KEITH DARRANT'S study. A large, dark-curtained room where the light from a single reading-lamp falling on Turkey carpet, on books beside a large armchair, on the deep blue-and-gold coffee service, makes a sort of oasis before a log fire. In red Turkish slippers and an old brown velvet coat, KEITH DARRANT sits asleep. He has a dark, clean-cut, clean-shaven face, dark grizzling hair, dark twisting eyebrows.]

[The curtained door away out in the dim part of the room behind him is opened so softly that he does not wake. LARRY DARRANT enters and stands half lost in the curtain over the door. A thin figure, with a worn, high cheek-boned face, deep-sunk blue eyes and wavy hair all ruffled—a face which still has a certain beauty. He moves inwards along the wall, stands still again and utters a gasping sigh. KEITH stirs in his chair.]

KEITH: Who's there?

LARRY: *[In a stifled voice]* Only I—Larry.

KEITH: *[Half-waked]* Come in! I was asleep. *[He does not turn his head, staring sleepily at the fire.]*

> *[The sound of LARRY's breathing can be heard.]*

KEITH: *[Turning his head a little]* Well, Larry, what is it?

> *[LARRY comes skirting along the wall, as if craving its support, outside the radius of the light.]*

KEITH: *[Staring]* Are you ill?

> *[LARRY stands still again and heaves a deep sigh.]*

KEITH: *[Rising, with his back to the fire, and staring at his brother]* What is it, man? *[Then with a brutality born of nerves suddenly ruffled]* Have you committed a murder that you stand there like a fish?

LARRY: *[In a whisper]* Yes, Keith.

KEITH: *[With vigorous disgust]* By Jove! Drunk again*! [In a voice changed by sudden apprehension]* What do you mean by coming here in this state? I told you— If you weren't my brother—! Come here, where I can see you! What's the matter with you, Larry?

> *[With a lurch LARRY leaves the shelter of the wall and sinks into a chair in the circle of light.]*

LARRY: It's true.

> *[KEITH steps quickly forward and stares down into his brother's eyes, where is a horrified wonder, as if they would never again get on terms with his face.]*

KEITH: *[Angry, bewildered-in a low voice]* What in God's name is this nonsense?
> *[He goes quickly over to the door and draws the curtain aside, to see that it is shut, then comes back to LARRY, who is huddling over the fire.]*
Come, Larry! Pull yourself together and drop exaggeration! What on earth do you mean?

LARRY: *[In a shrill outburst]* It's true, I tell you; I've killed a man.

KEITH: [Bracing himself; coldly] Be quiet!

> *[LARRY lifts his hands and wrings them.]*

KEITH: *[Utterly taken aback]* Why come here and tell me this?

LARRY: Whom should I tell, Keith? I came to ask what I'm to do—give myself up, or what?

KEITH: When—when—what—?

LARRY: Last night.

KEITH: Good God! How? Where? You'd better tell me quietly from the beginning. Here, drink this coffee; it'll clear your head.

    [He pours out and hands him a cup of coffee. LARRY drinks it off.]

LARRY: My head! Yes! It's like this, Keith—there's a girl—

KEITH: Women! Always women, with you! Well?

LARRY: A Polish girl. She—her father died over here when she was sixteen, and left her all alone. There was a mongrel living in the same house who married her—or pretended to. She's very pretty, Keith. He left her with a baby coming. She lost it, and nearly starved. Then another fellow took her on, and she lived with him two years, till that brute turned up again and made her go back to him. He used to beat her black and blue. He'd left her again when—I met her. She was taking anybody then. *[He stops, passes his hand over his lips, looks up at KEITH, and goes on defiantly]* I never met a sweeter woman, or a truer, that I swear. Woman! She's only twenty now! When I went to her last night, that devil had found her out again. He came for me—a bullying, great, hulking brute. Look! *[He touches a dark mark on his forehead]* I took his ugly throat, and when I let go— *[He stops and his hands drop.]*

KEITH: Yes?

LARRY: *[In a smothered voice]* Dead, Keith. I never knew till afterwards that she was hanging on to him—to h-help me. *[Again he wrings his hands.]*

KEITH: *[In a hard, dry voice]* What did you do then?

LARRY: We—we sat by it a long time.

KEITH: Well?

LARRY: Then I carried it on my back down the street, round a corner, to an archway.

KEITH: How far?

LARRY: About fifty yards.

KEITH: Was—did anyone see?

LARRY: No.

KEITH: What time?

LARRY: Three in the morning.

KEITH: And then?

LARRY: Went back to her.

KEITH: Why—in heaven's name?

LARRY: She way lonely and afraid. So was I, Keith.

KEITH: Where is this place?

LARRY: Forty-two Borrow Square, Soho.

KEITH: And the archway?

LARRY: Corner of Glove Lane.

KEITH: Good God! Why, I saw it in the paper this morning. They were talking of it in the Courts! *[He snatches the evening paper from his armchair, and runs it over and reads]* Here it is again. "Body of a man was found this morning under an archway in Glove Lane. From marks about the throat grave suspicion of foul play are entertained. The body had apparently been robbed." My God! *[Suddenly he turns]* You saw this in the paper and dreamed it. D'you understand, Larry?—you dreamed it.

LARRY: *[Wistfully]* If only I had, Keith!

> *[KEITH makes a movement of his hands almost like his brother's.]*

KEITH: Did you take anything from the—body?

LARRY: *[Drawing au envelope from his pocket]* This dropped out while we were struggling.

KEITH: *[Snatching it and reading]* "Patrick Walenn"—Was that his name? "Simon's Hotel, Farrier Street, London." *[Stooping, he puts it in the fire]* No!—that makes me— *[He bends to pluck it out, stays his hand, and stamps it suddenly further in with his foot]* What in God's name made you come here and tell me? Don't you know I'm—I'm within an ace of a Judgeship?

LARRY: *[Simply]* Yes. You must know what I ought to do. I didn't, mean to kill him, Keith. I love the girl—I love her. What shall I do?

KEITH: Love!

LARRY: *[In a flash]* Love!—That swinish brute! A million creatures die every day, and not one of them deserves death as he did. But—but I feel it here. *[Touching his heart]* Such an awful clutch, Keith. Help me if you can, old man. I may be no good, but I've never hurt a fly if I could help it. *[He buries his face in his hands.]*

KEITH: Steady, Larry! Let's think it out. You weren't seen, you say?

LARRY: It's a dark place, and dead night.

KEITH: When did you leave the girl again?

LARRY: About seven.

KEITH: Where did you go?

LARRY: To my rooms.

KEITH: To Fitzroy Street?

LARRY: Yes.

KEITH: What have you done since?

LARRY: Sat there—thinking.

KEITH: Not been out?

LARRY: No.

KEITH: Not seen the girl? *[LARRY shakes his head.]* Will she give you away?

LARRY: Never.

KEITH: Or herself—hysteria?

LARRY: No.

KEITH: Who knows of your relations with her?

LARRY: No one.

KEITH: No one?

LARRY: I don't know who should, Keith.

KEITH: Did anyone see you go in last night, when you first went to her?

LARRY: No. She lives on the ground floor. I've got keys.

KEITH: Give them to me.
  [LARRY takes two keys from his pocket and hands them to his brother.]

LARRY: *[Rising]* I can't be cut off from her!

KEITH: What! A girl like that?

LARRY: *[With a flash]* Yes, a girl like that.

KEITH: *[Moving his hand to put down old emotion]* What else have you that connects you with her?

LARRY: Nothing.

KEITH: In your rooms? *[LARRY shakes his head.]* Photographs? Letters?

LARRY: No.

KEITH: Sure?

LARRY: Nothing.

KEITH: No one saw you going back to her? *[LARRY shakes his head.]* Nor leave in the morning? You can't be certain.

LARRY: I am.

KEITH: You were fortunate. Sit down again, man. I must think.
> *[He turns to the fire and leans his elbows on the mantelpiece and his head on his hands. LARRY sits down again obediently.]*

KEITH: It's all too unlikely. It's monstrous!

LARRY: *[Sighing it out]* Yes.

KEITH: This Walenn--was it his first reappearance after an absence?

LARRY: Yes.

KEITH: How did he find out where she was?

LARRY: I don't know.

KEITH: *[Brutally]* How drunk were you?

LARRY: I was not drunk.

KEITH: How much had you drunk, then?

LARRY: A little claret—nothing!

KEITH: You say you didn't mean to kill him.

LARRY: God knows.

KEITH: That's something.

LARRY: He hit me. *[He holds up his hands]* I didn't know I was so strong.

KEITH: She was hanging on to him, you say?—That's ugly.

LARRY: She was scared for me.

KEITH: D'you mean she—loves you?

LARRY: *[Simply]* Yes, Keith.

KEITH: *[Brutally]* Can a woman like that love?

LARRY: *[Flashing out]* By God, you are a stony devil! Why not?

KEITH: *[Dryly]* I'm trying to get at truth. If you want me to help, I must know everything. What makes you think she's fond of you?

LARRY: *[With a crazy laugh]* Oh, you lawyer! Were you never in a woman's arms?

KEITH: I'm talking of love.

LARRY: *[Fiercely]* So am I. I tell you she's devoted. Did you ever pick up a lost dog? Well, she has the lost dog's love for me. And I for her; we picked each other up. I've never felt for another woman what I feel for her—she's been the saving of me!

KEITH: *[With a shrug]* What made you choose that archway?

LARRY: It was the first dark place.

KEITH: Did his face look as if he'd been strangled?

LARRY: Don't!

KEITH: Did it? *[LARRY bows his head.]* Very disfigured?

LARRY: Yes.

KEITH: Did you look to see if his clothes were marked?

LARRY: No.

KEITH: Why not?

LARRY: *[In an outburst]* I'm not made of iron, like you. Why not? If you had done it—!

KEITH: *[Holding up his hand]* You say he was disfigured. Would he be recognisable?

LARRY: *[Wearily]* I don't know.

KEITH: When she lived with him last—where was that?

LARRY: In Pimlico, I think.

KEITH: Not Soho? *[LARRY shakes his head.]* How long has she been at this Soho place?

LARRY: Nearly a year.

KEITH: Living this life?

LARRY: Till she met me.

KEITH: Till, she met you? And you believe—?

LARRY: *[Starting up]* Keith!

KEITH: *[Again raising his hand]* Always in the same rooms?

LARRY: *[Subsiding]* Yes.

KEITH: What was he? A professional bully? *[LARRY nods.]* Spending most of his time abroad, I suppose.

LARRY: I think so.

KEITH: Can you say if he was known to the police?

LARRY: I've never heard.
> *[KEITH turns away and walks up and down; then, stopping at LARRY's chair, he speaks.]*

KEITH: Now listen, Larry. When you leave here, go straight home, and stay there till I give you leave to go out again. Promise.

LARRY: I promise.

KEITH: Is your promise worth anything?

LARRY: *[With one of his flashes]* "Unstable as water, he shall not excel!"

KEITH: Exactly. But if I'm to help you, you must do as I say. I must have time to think this out. Have you got money?

LARRY: Very little.

KEITH: *[Grimly]* Half-quarter day—yes, your quarter's always spent by then. If you're to get away—never mind, I can manage the money.

LARRY: *[Humbly]* You're very good, Keith; you've always been very good to me—I don't know why.

KEITH: *[Sardonically]* Privilege of A brother. As it happens, I'm thinking of myself and our family. You can't indulge yourself in killing without bringing ruin. My God! I suppose you realise that you've made me an accessory after the fact—me, King's counsel—sworn to the service of the Law, who, in a year or two, will have the trying of cases like yours! By heaven, Larry, you've surpassed yourself!

LARRY: *[Bringing out a little box]* I'd better have done with it.

KEITH: You fool! Give that to me.

LARRY: *[With a strange smile]* No. *[He holds up a tabloid between finger and thumb]* White magic, Keith! Just one—and they may do what they like to you, and you won't know it. Snap your fingers at all the tortures. It's a great comfort! Have one to keep by you?

KEITH: Come, Larry! Hand it over.

LARRY: *[Replacing the box]* Not quite! You've never killed a man, you see. *[He gives that crazy laugh.]* D'you remember that hammer when we were boys and you riled me, up in the long room? I had luck then. I had luck in Naples once. I nearly killed a driver for beating his poor brute of a horse. But now—! My God! *[He covers his face.]*
         [KEITH touched, goes up and lays a hand on his shoulder.]

KEITH: Come, Larry! Courage!

[LARRY looks up at him.]

LARRY: All right, Keith; I'll try.

KEITH: Don't go out. Don't drink. Don't talk. Pull yourself together!

LARRY: *[Moving towards the door]* Don't keep me longer than you can help, Keith.

KEITH: No, no. Courage!
[LARRY reaches the door, turns as if to say something—finds no words, and goes.]

KEITH: *[To the fire]* Courage! My God! I shall need it!

CURTAIN

SCENE II. Wanda's room.

[About eleven o'clock the following night in WANDA'S room on the ground floor in Soho. In the light from one close-shaded electric bulb the room is but dimly visible. A dying fire burns on the left. A curtained window in the centre of the back wall. A door on the right. The furniture is plush-covered and commonplace, with a kind of shabby smartness. A couch, without back or arms, stands aslant, between window and fire.]

[On this WANDA is sitting, her knees drawn up under her, staring at the embers. She has on only her nightgown and a wrapper over it; her bare feet are thrust into slippers. Her hands are crossed and pressed over her breast. She starts and looks up, listening. Her eyes are candid and startled, her face alabaster pale, and its pale brown hair, short and square-cut, curls towards her bare neck. The startled dark eyes and the faint rose of her lips are like colour-staining on a white mask.]

[Footsteps as of a policeman, very measured, pass on the pavement outside, and die away. She gets up and steals to the window, draws one curtain aside so that a chink of the night is seen. She opens the curtain wider, till the shape of a bare, witch-like tree becomes visible in the open space of the little Square on the far side of the road. The footsteps are heard once more coming nearer. WANDA closes the curtains and cranes back. They pass and die again. She moves away and looking down at the floor between door and couch, as though seeing something there; shudders; covers her eyes; goes back to the couch and down again just as before, to stare at the embers. Again she is startled by noise of the outer door being opened. She springs up, runs and turns the light by a switch close to the door. By the glimmer of the fire she can just be seen standing by the dark window-curtains, listening. There comes the sound of subdued knocking on her door. She stands in breathless terror. The knocking is repeated. The sound of a latchkey in the door is heard. Her terror leaves her. The door opens; a man enters in a dark, fur overcoat.]

WANDA: *[In a voice of breathless relief, with a rather foreign accent]* Oh!
It's you, Larry! Why did you knock? I was so frightened. Come in! *[She*

crosses quickly, and flings her arms round his neck—then recoiling, in a terror-stricken whisper] Oh! Who is it?

KEITH: *[In a smothered voice]* A friend of Larry's. Don't be frightened.
    [She has recoiled again to the window; and when he finds the switch and turns the light up, she is seen standing there holding her dark wrapper up to her throat, so that her face has an uncanny look of being detached from the body.]

KEITH: *[Gently]* You needn't be afraid. I haven't come to do you harm— quite the contrary. *[Holding up the keys]* Larry wouldn't have given me these, would he, if he hadn't trusted me?
    [WANDA does not move, staring like a spirit startled out of the flesh.]

KEITH: *[After looking round him]* I'm sorry to have startled you.

WANDA: *[In a whisper]* Who are you, please?

KEITH: Larry's brother.
    [WANDA, with a sigh of utter relief, steals forward to the couch and sinks down. KEITH goes up to her.]
He'd told me.

WANDA: *[Clasping her hands round her knees.]* Yes?

KEITH: An awful business!

WANDA: Yes; oh, yes! Awful—it is awful!

KEITH: *[Staring round him again.]* In this room?

WANDA: Just where you are standing. I see him now, always falling.

KEITH: *[Moved by the gentle despair in her voice]* You—look very young. What's your name?

WANDA: Wanda.

KEITH: Are you fond of Larry?

WANDA: I would die for him!

[A moment's silence.]

KEITH: I—I've come to see what you can do to save him.

WANDA: *[Wistfully]* You would not deceive me. You are really his brother?

KEITH: I swear it.

WANDA: *[Clasping her hands]* If I can save him! Won't you sit down?

KEITH: *[Drawing up a chair and sitting]* This, man, your—your husband, before he came here the night before last—how long since you saw him?

WANDA: Eighteen month.

KEITH: Does anyone about here know you are his wife?

WANDA: No. I came here to live a bad life. Nobody know me. I am quite alone.

KEITH: They've discovered who he was—you know that?

WANDA: No; I have not dared to go out.

KEITH: Well, they have; and they'll look for anyone connected with him, of course.

WANDA: He never let people think I was married to him. I don't know if I was—really. We went to an office and signed our names; but he was a wicked man. He treated many, I think, like me.

KEITH: Did my brother ever see him before?

WANDA: Never! And that man first went for him.

KEITH: Yes. I saw the mark. Have you a servant?

WANDA: No. A woman come at nine in the morning for an hour.

KEITH: Does she know Larry?

WANDA: No. He is always gone.

KEITH: Friends—acquaintances?

WANDA: No; I am verree quiet. Since I know your brother, I see no one, sare.

KEITH: *[Sharply]* Do you mean that?

WANDA: Oh, yes! I love him. Nobody come here but him for a long time now.

KEITH: How long?

WANDA: Five month.

KEITH: So you have not been out since—? *[WANDA shakes her head.]* What have you been doing?

WANDA: *[Simply]* Crying. *[Pressing her hands to her breast]* He is in danger because of me. I am so afraid for him.

KEITH: *[Checking her emotion]* Look at me. *[She looks at him.]* If the worst comes, and this man is traced to you, can you trust yourself not to give Larry away?

WANDA: *[Rising and pointing to the fire]* Look! I have burned all the things he have given me—even his picture. Now I have nothing from him.

KEITH: *[Who has risen too]* Good! One more question. Do the police know you—because—of your life?
        [She looks at him intently, and shakes her, head.]
You know where Larry lives?

WANDA: Yes.

KEITH: You mustn't go there, and he mustn't come to you.
        [She bows her head; then, suddenly comes close to him.]

WANDA: Please do not take him from me altogether. I will be so careful. I will not do anything to hurt him. But if I cannot see him sometimes, I shall die. Please do not take him from me.

[She catches his hand and presses it desperately between her own.]

KEITH: Leave that to me. I'm going to do all I can.

WANDA: *[Looking up into his face]* But you will be kind?
[Suddenly she bends and kisses his hand. KEITH draws his hand away, and she recoils a little humbly, looking up at him again. Suddenly she stands rigid, listening.]

WANDA: *[In a whisper]* Listen! Someone—out there!
[She darts past him and turns out the light. There is a knock on the door. They are now close together between door and window.]

WANDA: *[Whispering]* Oh! Who is it?

KEITH: *[Under his breath]* You said no one comes but Larry.

WANDA: Yes, and you have his keys. Oh! if it is Larry! I must open!
[KEITH shrinks back against the wall. WANDA goes to the door.]

WANDA: *[Opening the door an inch]* Yes? Please? Who?
[A thin streak of light from a bull's-eye lantern outside plays over the wall. A Policeman's voice says: "All right, Miss. Your outer door's open. You ought to keep it shut after dark, you know."]
Thank you, sir.
[The sound of retreating footsteps, of the outer door closing. WANDA shuts the door.]
A policeman!

KEITH: *[Moving from the wall]* Curse! I must have left that door.
[Suddenly-turning up the light] You told me they didn't know you.

WANDA: *[Sighing]* I did not think they did, sir. It is so long I was not out in the town; not since I had Larry.
[KEITH gives her an intent look, then crosses to the fire. He stands there a moment, looking down, then turns to the girl, who has crept back to the couch.]

KEITH: *[Half to himself]* After your life, who can believe—? Look here! You drifted together and you'll drift apart, you know. Better for him to get away and make a clean cut of it.

WANDA: *[Uttering a little moaning sound]* Oh, sir! May I not love, because I have been bad? I was only sixteen when that man spoiled me. If you knew—

KEITH: I'm thinking of Larry. With you, his danger is much greater. There's a good chance as things are going. You may wreck it. And for what? Just a few months more of—well—you know.

WANDA: *[Standing at the head of the couch and touching her eyes with her hands]* Oh, sir! Look! It is true. He is my life. Don't take him away from me.

KEITH: *[Moved and restless]* You must know what Larry is. He'll never stick to you.

WANDA: *[Simply]* He will, sir.

KEITH: *[Energetically]* The last man on earth to stick to anything! But for the sake of a whim he'll risk his life and the honour of all his family. I know him.

WANDA: No, no, you do not. It is I who know him.

KEITH: Now, now! At any moment they may find out your connection with that man. So long as Larry goes on with you, he's tied to this murder, don't you see?

WANDA: *[Coming close to him]* But he love me. Oh, sir! he love me!

KEITH: Larry has loved dozens of women.

WANDA: Yes, but— *[Her face quivers]*.

KEITH: *[Brusquely]* Don't cry! If I give you money, will you disappear, for his sake?

WANDA: *[With a moan]* It will be in the water, then. There will be no cruel men there.

KEITH: Ah! First Larry, then you! Come now. It's better for you both. A few months, and you'll forget you ever met.

WANDA: *[Looking wildly up]* I will go if Larry say I must. But not to live. No! *[Simply]* I could not, sir. [KEITH, moved, is silent.] I could not live without Larry. What is left for a girl like me—when she once love? It is finish.

KEITH: I don't want you to go back to that life.

WANDA: No; you do not care what I do. Why should you? I tell you I will go if Larry say I must.

KEITH: That's not enough. You know that. You must take it out of his hands. He will never give up his present for the sake of his future. If you're as fond of him as you say, you'll help to save him.

WANDA: *[Below her breath]* Yes! Oh, yes! But do not keep him long from me—I beg! *[She sinks to the floor and clasps his knees.]*

KEITH: Well, well! Get up. *[There is a tap on the window-pane]* Listen! *[A faint, peculiar whistle.]*

WANDA: *[Springing up]* Larry! Oh, thank God!
          *[She runs to the door, opens it, and goes out to bring him in.
          KEITH stands waiting, facing the open doorway.]*

          [LARRY entering with WANDA just behind him.]

LARRY: Keith!

KEITH: *[Grimly]* So much for your promise not to go out!

LARRY: I've been waiting in for you all day. I couldn't stand it any longer.

KEITH: Exactly!

LARRY: Well, what's the sentence, brother? Transportation for life and then to be fined forty pounds?

KEITH: So you can joke, can you?

LARRY: Must.

KEITH: A boat leaves for the Argentine the day after to-morrow; you must go by it.

LARRY: *[Putting his arms round WANDA, who is standing motionless with her eyes fixed on him]* Together, Keith?

KEITH: You can't go together. I'll send her by the next boat.

LARRY: Swear?

KEITH: Yes. You're lucky they're on a false scent.

LARRY: What?

KEITH: You haven't seen it?

LARRY: I've seen nothing, not even a paper.

KEITH: They've taken up a vagabond who robbed the body. He pawned a snake-shaped ring, and they identified this Walenn by it. I've been down and seen him charged myself.

LARRY: With murder?

WANDA: *[Faintly]* Larry!

KEITH: He's in no danger. They always get the wrong man first. It'll do him no harm to be locked up a bit—hyena like that. Better in prison, anyway, than sleeping out under archways in this weather.

LARRY: What was he like, Keith?

KEITH: A little yellow, ragged, lame, unshaven scarecrow of a chap. They were fools to think he could have had the strength.

LARRY: What! *[In an awed voice]* Why, I saw him—after I left you last night.

KEITH: You? Where?

LARRY: By the archway.

KEITH: You went back there?

LARRY: It draws you, Keith.

KEITH: You're mad, I think.

LARRY: I talked to him, and he said, "Thank you for this little chat. It's worth more than money when you're down." Little grey man like a shaggy animal. And a newspaper boy came up and said: "That's right, guv'nors! 'Ere's where they found the body—very spot. They 'yn't got 'im yet."
        [He laughs; and the terrified girl presses herself against him.]
An innocent man!

KEITH: He's in no danger, I tell you. He could never have strangled—Why, he hadn't the strength of a kitten. Now, Larry! I'll take your berth to-morrow. Here's money *[He brings out a pile of notes and puts them on the couch]* You can make a new life of it out there together presently, in the sun.

LARRY: *[In a whisper]* In the sun! "A cup of wine and thou." *[Suddenly]* How can I, Keith? I must see how it goes with that poor devil.

KEITH: Bosh! Dismiss it from your mind; there's not nearly enough evidence.

LARRY: Not?

KEITH: No. You've got your chance. Take it like a man.

LARRY: *[With a strange smile—to the girl]* Shall we, Wanda?

WANDA: Oh, Larry!

LARRY: *[Picking the notes up from the couch]* Take them back, Keith.

KEITH: What! I tell you no jury would convict; and if they did, no judge would hang. A ghoul who can rob a dead body, ought to be in prison. He did worse than you.

LARRY: It won't do, Keith. I must see it out.

KEITH: Don't be a fool!

LARRY: I've still got some kind of honour. If I clear out before I know, I shall have none—nor peace. Take them, Keith, or I'll put them in the fire.

KEITH: *[Taking back the notes; bitterly]* I suppose I may ask you not to be entirely oblivious of our name. Or is that unworthy of your honour?

LARRY: *[Hanging his head]* I'm awfully sorry, Keith; awfully sorry, old man.

KEITH: *[sternly]* You owe it to me—to our name—to our dead mother—to do nothing anyway till we see what happens.

LARRY: I know. I'll do nothing without you, Keith.

KEITH: *[Taking up his hat]* Can I trust you? *[He stares hard at his brother.]*

LARRY: You can trust me.

KEITH: Swear?

LARRY: I swear.

KEITH: Remember, nothing! Good night!

LARRY: Good night!
> *[KEITH goes. LARRY sits down on the couch and stares at the fire. The girl steals up and slips her arms about him.]*

LARRY: An innocent man!

WANDA: Oh, Larry! But so are you. What did we want—to kill that man? Never! Oh! kiss me!
> *[LARRY turns his face. She kisses his lips.]*
I have suffered so—not seein' you. Don't leave me again—don't! Stay here. Isn't it good to be together?—Oh! Poor Larry! How tired you look!—Stay with me. I am so frightened all alone. So frightened they will take you from me.

LARRY: Poor child!

WANDA: No, no! Don't look like that!

LARRY: You're shivering.

WANDA: I will make up the fire. Love me, Larry! I want to forget.

LARRY: The poorest little wretch on God's earth—locked up—for me! A little wild animal, locked up. There he goes, up and down, up and down—in his cage—don't you see him?—looking for a place to gnaw his way through—little grey rat. *[He gets up and roams about.]*

WANDA: No, no! I can't bear it! Don't frighten me more!
        [He comes back and takes her in his arms.]

LARRY: There, there! *[He kisses her closed eyes.]*

WANDA: *[Without moving]* If we could sleep a little—wouldn't it be nice?

LARRY: Sleep?

WANDA: *[Raising herself]* Promise to stay with me—to stay here for good, Larry. I will cook for you; I will make you so comfortable. They will find him innocent. And then—Oh, Larry! in the sun—right away—far from this horrible country. How lovely! *[Trying to get him to look at her]* Larry!

LARRY: [With a movement to free 'himself] To the edge of the world— and—over!

WANDA: No, no! No, no! You don't want me to die, Larry, do you? I shall if you leave me. Let us be happy! Love me!

LARRY: *[With a laugh]* Ah! Let's be happy and shut out the sight of him. Who cares? Millions suffer for no mortal reason. Let's be strong, like Keith. No! I won't leave you, Wanda. Let's forget everything except ourselves. *[Suddenly]* There he goes-up and down!

WANDA: *[Moaning]* No, no! See! I will pray to the Virgin. She will pity us!

*[She falls on her knees and clasps her hands, praying. Her lips
move. LARRY stands motionless, with arms crossed, and on his
face are yearning and mockery, love and despair.]*

LARRY: *[Whispering]* Pray for us! Bravo! Pray away!
    *[Suddenly the girl stretches out her arms and lifts her face with a
    look of ecstasy.]*
What?

WANDA: She is smiling! We shall be happy soon.

LARRY: *[Bending down over her]* Poor child! When we die, Wanda, let's
go together. We should keep each other warm out in the dark.

WANDA: *[Raising her hands to his face]* Yes! oh, yes! If you die I could
not—I could not go on living!

CURTAIN

SCENE III. Wanda's room. Two months later.

[WANDA'S room. Daylight is just beginning to fail of a January afternoon. The table is laid for supper, with decanters of wine.]

[WANDA is standing at the window looking out at the wintry trees of the Square beyond the pavement. A newspaper Boy's voice is heard coming nearer.]

VOICE: Pyper! Glove Lyne murder! Trial and verdict! *[Receding]* Verdict! Pyper!
> *[WANDA throws up the window as if to call to him, checks herself, closes it and runs to the door. She opens it, but recoils into the room. KEITH is standing there. He comes in.]*

KEITH: Where's Larry?

WANDA: He went to the trial. I could not keep him from it. The trial— Oh! what has happened, sir?

KEITH: *[Savagely]* Guilty! Sentence of death! Fools!—idiots!

WANDA: Of death! *[For a moment she seems about to swoon.]*

KEITH: Girl! girl! It may all depend on you. Larry's still living here?

WANDA: Yes.

KEITH: I must wait for him.

WANDA: Will you sit down, please?

KEITH: *[Shaking his head]* Are you ready to go away at any time?

WANDA: Yes, yes; always I am ready.

KEITH: And he?

WANDA: Yes—but now! What will he do? That poor man!

KEITH: A graveyard thief—a ghoul!

WANDA: Perhaps he was hungry. I have been hungry: you do things then that you would not. Larry has thought of him in prison so much all these weeks. Oh! what shall we do now?

KEITH: Listen! Help me. Don't let Larry out of your sight. I must see how things go. They'll never hang this wretch. *[He grips her arms]* Now, we must stop Larry from giving himself up. He's fool enough. D'you understand?

WANDA: Yes. But why has he not come in? Oh! If he have, already!

KEITH: *[Letting go her arms]* My God! If the police come—find me here— *[He moves to the door]* No, he wouldn't without seeing you first. He's sure to come. Watch him like a lynx. Don't let him go without you.

WANDA: *[Clasping her hands on her breast]* I will try, sir.

KEITH: Listen! *[A key is heard in the lock.]* It's he!
        *[LARRY enters. He is holding a great bunch of pink lilies and
        white narcissus. His face tells nothing. KEITH looks from him to
        the girl, who stands motionless.]*

LARRY: Keith! So you've seen?

KEITH: The thing can't stand. I'll stop it somehow. But you must give me time, Larry.

LARRY: *[Calmly]* Still looking after your honour, Keith?

KEITH: *[Grimly]* Think my reasons what you like.

WANDA: *[Softly]* Larry!
        [LARRY puts his arm round her.]

LARRY: Sorry, old man.

KEITH: This man can and shall get off. I want your solemn promise that you won't give yourself up, nor even go out till I've seen you again.

LARRY: I give it.

KEITH: *[Looking from one to the other]* By the memory of our mother, swear that.

LARRY: *[With a smile]* I swear.

KEITH: I have your oath—both of you—both of you. I'm going at once to see what can be done.

LARRY: *[Softly]* Good luck, brother.
            [KEITH goes out.]

WANDA: *[Putting her hands on LARRY's breast]* What does it mean?

LARRY: Supper, child—I've had nothing all day. Put these lilies in water.
            *[She takes the lilies and obediently puts them into a vase. LARRY
            pours wine into a deep-coloured glass and drinks it off.]*
We've had a good time, Wanda. Best time I ever had, these last two months; and nothing but the bill to pay.

WANDA: *[Clasping him desperately]* Oh, Larry! Larry!

LARRY: *[Holding her away to look at her.]* Take off those things and put on a bridal garment.

WANDA: Promise me—wherever you go, I go too. Promise! Larry, you think I haven't seen, all these weeks. But I have seen everything; all in your heart, always. You cannot hide from me. I knew—I knew! Oh, if we might go away into the sun! Oh! Larry—couldn't we? *[She searches his eyes with hers—then shuddering]* Well! If it must be dark—I don't care, if I may go in your arms. In prison we could not be together. I am ready. Only love me first. Don't let me cry before I go. Oh! Larry, will there be much pain?

LARRY: *[In a choked voice]* No pain, my pretty.

WANDA: *[With a little sigh]* It is a pity.

LARRY: If you had seen him, as I have, all day, being tortured. Wanda—we shall be out of it. *[The wine mounting to his head]* We shall be free in the dark; free of their cursed inhumanities. I hate this world—I loathe it! I hate its God-forsaken savagery; its pride and smugness! Keith's world—all righteous will-power and success. We're no good here, you and I—we were cast out at birth—soft, will-less—better dead. No fear, Keith! I'm staying indoors. *[He pours wine into two glasses]* Drink it up! *[Obediently WANDA drinks, and he also.]* Now go and make yourself beautiful.

WANDA: *[Seizing him in her arms]* Oh, Larry!

LARRY: *[Touching her face and hair]* Hanged by the neck until he's dead—for what I did.
> *[WANDA takes a long look at his face, slips her arms from him, and goes out through the curtains below the fireplace.]*

> *[LARRY feels in his pocket, brings out the little box, opens it, fingers the white tabloids.]*

LARRY: Two each--after food. *[He laughs and puts back the box]* Oh! my girl!
> *[The sound of a piano playing a faint festive tune is heard afar off. He mutters, staring at the fire.]*

Flames-flame, and flicker-ashes. "No more, no more, the moon is dead, And all the people in it."
> *[He sits on the couch with a piece of paper on his knees, adding a few words with a stylo pen to what is already written. The GIRL, in a silk wrapper, coming back through the curtains, watches him. He looks up.]*

It's all here—I've confessed. *[Reading]*

"Please bury us together."
"LAURENCE DARRANT.
"January 28th, about six p.m."

They'll find us in the morning. Come and have supper, my dear love.
> *[The girl creeps forward. He rises, puts his arm round her, and with her arm twined round him, smiling into each other's faces, they go to the table and sit down.]*

> *[The curtain falls for a few seconds to indicate the passage of three hours. When it rises again, the lovers are lying on the couch, in each other's arms, the lilies stream about them. The girl's bare arm is round LARRY'S neck. Her eyes are closed; his are open and sightless. There is no light but fire-light.]*

> *[A knocking on the door and the sound of a key turned in the lock. KEITH enters. He stands a moment bewildered by the half-light,*

then calls sharply: "Larry!" and turns up the light. Seeing the forms on the couch, he recoils a moment. Then, glancing at the table and empty decanters, goes up to the couch.]

KEITH: *[Muttering]* Asleep! Drunk! Ugh! *[Suddenly he bends, touches LARRY, and springs back.]* What! *[He bends again, shakes him and calls]* Larry! Larry! *[Then, motionless, he stares down at his brother's open, sightless eyes. Suddenly he wets his finger and holds it to the girl's lips, then to LARRY'S. He bends and listens at their hearts; catches sight of the little box lying between them and takes it up.]* My God! *[Then, raising himself, he closes his brother's eyes, and as he does so, catches sight of a paper pinned to the couch; detaches it and reads:]* "I, Lawrence Darrant, about to die by my own hand confess that I—" *[He reads on silently, in horror; finishes, letting the paper drop, and recoils from the couch on to a chair at the dishevelled supper table. Aghast, he sits there. Suddenly he mutters:]* If I leave that there—my name—my whole future! *[He springs up, takes up the paper again, and again reads.]* My God! It's ruin! *[He makes as if to tear it across, stops, and looks down at those two; covers his eyes with his hand; drops the paper and rushes to the door. But he stops there and comes back, magnetised, as it were, by that paper. He takes it up once more and thrusts it into his pocket. The footsteps of a Policeman pass, slow and regular, outside. His face crisps and quivers; he stands listening till they die away. Then he snatches the paper from his pocket, and goes past the foot of the couch to the fore.]* All my—No! Let him hang! *[He thrusts the paper into the fire, stamps it down with his foot, watches it writhe and blacken. Then suddenly clutching his head, he turns to the bodies on the couch. Panting and like a man demented, he recoils past the head of the couch, and rushing to the window, draws the curtains and throws the window up for air. Out in the darkness rises the witch-like skeleton tree, where a dark shape seems hanging. KEITH starts back.]* What's that? What—! *[He shuts the window and draws the dark curtains across it again.]* Fool! Nothing!

> *[Clenching his fists, he draws himself up, steadying himself with all his might. Then slowly he moves to the door, stands a second like a carved figure, his face hard as stone. Deliberately he turns out the light, opens the door, and goes. The still bodies lie there before the fire which is licking at the last blackened wafer.]*

CURTAIN

THE SUN

A SCENE

CHARACTERS

———✦———

THE GIRL
THE MAN
THE SOLDIER

THE SUN

[A Girl, sits crouched over her knees on a stile close to a river. A MAN with a silver badge stands beside her, clutching the worn top plank. THE GIRL'S level brows are drawn together; her eyes see her memories. THE MAN's eyes see THE GIRL; he has a dark, twisted face. The bright sun shines; the quiet river flows; the Cuckoo is calling; the mayflower is in bloom along the hedge that ends in the stile on the towing-path.]

THE GIRL: God knows what 'e'll say, Jim.

THE MAN: Let 'im. 'E's come too late, that's all.

THE GIRL: He couldn't come before. I'm frightened. 'E was fond o' me.

THE MAN: And aren't I fond of you?

THE GIRL: I ought to 'a waited, Jim; with 'im in the fightin'.

THE MAN: *[Passionately]* And what about me? Aren't I been in the fightin'—earned all I could get?

THE GIRL: *[Touching him]* Ah!

THE MAN: Did you—? *[He cannot speak the words.]*

THE GIRL: Not like you, Jim—not like you.

THE MAN: Have a spirit, then.

THE GIRL: I promised him.

THE MAN: One man's luck's another's poison.

THE GIRL: I ought to 'a waited. I never thought he'd come back from the fightin'.

THE MAN: *[Grimly]* Maybe 'e'd better not 'ave.

THE GIRL: *[Looking back along the tow-path]* What'll he be like, I wonder?

THE MAN: *[Gripping her shoulder]* Daisy, don't you never go back on me, or I should kill you, and 'im too.
          [THE GIRL looks at him, shivers, and puts her lips to his.]

THE GIRL: I never could.

THE MAN: Will you run for it? 'E'd never find us!
          [THE GIRL shakes her head.]

THE MAN: *[Dully]* What's the good o' stayin'? The world's wide.

THE GIRL: I'd rather have it off me mind, with him home.

THE MAN: *[Clenching his hands]* It's temptin' Providence.

THE GIRL: What's the time, Jim?

THE MAN: *[Glancing at the sun]* 'Alf past four.

THE GIRL: *[Looking along the towing-path]* He said four o'clock. Jim, you better go.

THE MAN: Not I. I've not got the wind up. I've seen as much of hell as he has, any day. What like is he?

THE GIRL: *[Dully]* I dunno, just. I've not seen him these three years. I dunno no more, since I've known you.

THE MAN: Big or little chap?

THE GIRL: 'Bout your size. Oh! Jim, go along!

THE MAN: No fear! What's a blighter like that to old Fritz's shells? We didn't shift when they was comin'. If you'll go, I'll go; not else.
          [Again she shakes her head.]

THE GIRL: Jim, do you love me true?
          [For answer THE MAN takes her avidly in his arms.]
I ain't ashamed—I ain't ashamed. If 'e could see me 'eart.

THE MAN: Daisy! If I'd known you out there, I never could 'a stuck it. They'd 'a got me for a deserter. That's how I love you!

THE GIRL: Jim, don't lift your hand to 'im! Promise!

THE MAN: That's according.

THE GIRL: Promise!

THE MAN: If 'e keeps quiet, I won't. But I'm not accountable—not always, I tell you straight—not since I've been through that.

THE GIRL: *[With a shiver]* Nor p'raps he isn't.

THE MAN: Like as not. It takes the lynch pins out, I tell you.

THE GIRL: God 'elp us!

THE MAN: *[Grimly]* Ah! We said that a bit too often. What we want we take, now; there's no one else to give it us, and there's no fear'll stop us; we seen the bottom of things.

THE GIRL: P'raps he'll say that too.

THE MAN: Then it'll be 'im or me.

THE GIRL: I'm frightened:

THE MAN: *[Tenderly]* No, Daisy, no! The river's handy. One more or less. 'E shan't 'arm you; nor me neither. *[He takes out a knife.]*

THE GIRL: *[Seizing his hand]* Oh, no! Give it to me, Jim!

THE MAN: *[Smiling]* No fear! *[He puts it away]* Shan't 'ave no need for it like as not. All right, little Daisy; you can't be expected to see things like what we do. What's life, anyway? I've seen a thousand lives taken in five minutes. I've seen dead men on the wires like flies on a flypaper. I've been as good as dead meself a hundred times. I've killed a dozen men. It's nothin'. He's safe, if 'e don't get my blood up. If he does, nobody's safe; not 'im, nor anybody else; not even you. I'm speakin' sober.

THE GIRL: *[Softly]* Jim, you won't go fightin' in the sun, with the birds all callin'?

THE MAN: That depends on 'im. I'm not lookin' for it. Daisy, I love you. I love your hair. I love your eyes. I love you.

THE GIRL: And I love you, Jim. I don't want nothin' more than you in all the world.

THE MAN: Amen to that, my dear. Kiss me close!
> *[The sound of a voice singing breaks in on their embrace. THE GIRL starts from his arms, and looks behind her along the towing-path. THE MAN draws back against, the hedge, fingering his side, where the knife is hidden. The song comes nearer.]*

> "I'll be right there to-night,
> Where the fields are snowy white;
> Banjos ringing, darkies singing,
> All the world seems bright."

THE GIRL: It's him!

THE MAN: Don't get the wind up, Daisy. I'm here!
> *[The singing stops. A man's voice says "Christ! It's Daisy; it's little Daisy 'erself!" THE GIRL stands rigid. The figure of a soldier appears on the other side of the stile. His cap is tucked into his belt, his hair is bright in the sunshine; he is lean, wasted, brown, and laughing.]*

SOLDIER: Daisy! Daisy! Hallo, old pretty girl!
> *[THE GIRL does not move, barring the way, as it were.]*

THE GIRL: Hallo, Jack! *[Softly]* I got things to tell you!

SOLDIER: What sort o' things, this lovely day? Why, I got things that'd take me years to tell. Have you missed me, Daisy?

THE GIRL: You been so long.

SOLDIER: So I 'ave. My Gawd! It's a way they 'ave in the Army. I said when I got out of it I'd laugh. Like as the sun itself I used to think of you, Daisy, when the trumps was comin' over, and the wind was up. D'you

remember that last night in the wood? "Come back and marry me quick,
Jack." Well, here I am—got me pass to heaven. No more fightin', no more
drillin', no more sleepin' rough. We can get married now, Daisy. We can
live soft an' 'appy. Give us a kiss, my dear.

THE GIRL: *[Drawing back]* No.

SOLDIER: *[Blankly]* Why not?
      *[THE MAN, with a swift movement steps along the hedge to THE
      GIRL'S side.]*

THE MAN: That's why, soldier.

SOLDIER: *[Leaping over the stile]* 'Oo are you, Pompey? The sun don't
shine in your inside, do it? 'Oo is he, Daisy?

THE GIRL: My man.

SOLDIER: Your-man! Lummy! "Taffy was a Welshman, Taffy was a
thief!" Well, mate! So you've been through it, too. I'm laughin' this
mornin' as luck will 'ave it. Ah! I can see your knife.

THE MAN: *[Who has half drawn his knife]* Don't laugh at me, I tell you.

SOLDIER: Not at you, not at you. *[He looks from one to the other]* I'm
laughin' at things in general. Where did you get it, mate?

THE MAN: *[Watchfully]* Through the lung.

SOLDIER: Think o' that! An' I never was touched. Four years an' never
was touched. An' so you've come an' took my girl! Nothin' doin'! Ha!
[Again he looks from one to the other-then away] Well! The world's before
me! *[He laughs]* I'll give you Daisy for a lung protector.

THE MAN: *[Fiercely]* You won't. I've took her.

SOLDIER: That's all right, then. You keep 'er. I've got a laugh in me you
can't put out, black as you look! Good-bye, little Daisy!
      [THE GIRL makes a movement towards him.]

THE MAN: Don't touch 'im!
      [THE GIRL stands hesitating, and suddenly bursts into tears.]

SOLDIER: Look 'ere, mate; shake 'ands! I don't want to see a girl cry, this day of all, with the sun shinin'. I seen too much of sorrer. You and me've been at the back of it. We've 'ad our whack. Shake!

THE MAN: Who are you kiddin'? You never loved 'er!

SOLDIER: *[After a long moment's pause]* Oh! I thought I did.

THE MAN: I'll fight you for her.
        [He drops his knife.]

SOLDIER: *[Slowly]* Mate, you done your bit, an' I done mine. It's took us two ways, seemin'ly.

THE GIRL: *[Pleading]* Jim!

THE MAN: *[With clenched fists]* I don't want 'is charity. I only want what I can take.

SOLDIER: Daisy, which of us will you 'ave?

THE GIRL: *[Covering her face]* Oh! Him!

SOLDIER: You see, mate! Put your 'ands down. There's nothin' for it but a laugh. You an' me know that. Laugh, mate!

THE MAN: You blarsted—!
        [THE GIRL springs to him and stops his mouth.]

SOLDIER: It's no use, mate. I can't do it. I said I'd laugh to-day, and laugh I will. I've come through that, an' all the stink of it; I've come through sorrer. Never again! Cheerio, mate! The sun's a-shinin'! He turns away.

THE GIRL: Jack, don't think too 'ard of me!

SOLDIER: *[Looking back]* No fear, my dear! Enjoy your fancy! So long! Gawd bless you both!
        [He sings, and goes along the path, and the song fades away.]

"I'll be right there to-night
　Where the fields are snowy white;
　Banjos ringing, darkies singing
　All the world seems bright!"

THE MAN: 'E's mad!

THE GIRL: *[Looking down the path with her hands clasped]* The sun has touched 'im, Jim!

CURTAIN

MORE BOOKS FROM BLACK BOX PRESS

Dialogues of the Dead
by BAUDELAIRE JONES

Lord Byron: Six Plays
by GEORGE GORDON BYRON

Prometheus Unbound
by PERCY BYSSHE SHELLEY

Three Plays of the Absurd
by WALTER WYKES

He Who Gets Slapped and Other Plays
by LEONID ANDREYEV

Royalty-Free One-Act Plays
by J. CRABB

Ten 10-Minute Plays
by WALTER WYKES